Reconstructing Charlie

By

Charmaine Gordon

Vanilla Heart Publishing

USA

Reconstructing Charlie

by Charmaine Gordon

Copyright 2011 Charmaine Gordon

Published by: Vanilla Heart Publishing
www.VanillaHeartBooksAndAuthors.com
10121 Evergreen Way, 25-156
Everett, WA 98204 USA

ISBN-13: 978-0615909172   ISBN-10: 0615909175

10 9 8 7 6 5 4 3 2 Second Edition

First Printing, October 2013
Printed in the United States of America

Reconstructing Charlie

By

Charmaine Gordon

Dedication

To Kimberlee Williams, my publisher, who said 'tell me a story' and proceeded to help me hammer out a solid story from my sleep writing idea, I give grateful thanks.

And to daughter Amy Malone who, when hearing about the new book, reminded me 'the readers should love her, Mom.' She also came up with the title "RECONSTRUCTING CHARLIE" Thank you, dear only daughter o' mine.

Just in time, I joined the Tuesday night critique group and these talented writers steered me in the right direction during the early phase of my new story. I learned so much from Janet Lane Walters, Gianna Simone, Claire Ruane, Elf Ahearn, Kat Attalla, Liz Matis, and Yolanda Sly as we munched our way through stimulating meetings.

Author Malcolm R. Campbell won the name the grandmother contest with his entry of Granny Apple and thus the lovely Irish chef came to be.

A very special thank you to April Likhite-Head Cross Country Coach-Northwestern University, Evanston, Illinois for her generosity in giving me time to explain workouts, training and the joy of running. Keeping in mind this is a tale coming from my imagination and set within NU, Evanston, cross country track, an inspiring coach, and a young woman at the center of it all, any errors I've made are mine.

Prologue

In 1996, I killed my father.

Dear old Dad was great with a belt. A belt of whiskey. A belt from around his waist unbuckled when you least expected it and later I knew when it was coming and some of us escaped. Not me, not Mom. Never Mom. I'm the oldest. I didn't want the little ones to see the okay dad turn into a monster dad on payday. Every payday.

Chapter 1

I heard the television turned up loud before I opened the door. Mom always hoped for a distraction. Maybe this time instead of beating up on us, he'd watch the Minnesota Twins beat the hell out of the Boston Red Sox. Rant over every play, curse the umpires, yell that the Hubert H. Humphrey Stadium wasn't good enough. 1996. Not a great year so far for the Twins. On this payday, after I dropped the kids off, I raced home just in time to be with Mom.

The front door banged open hard enough to rattle dishes in the cabinet. Mom's treasure—a painted porcelain egg—rolled to the edge, teetered for a second and fell end over end to the hardwood floor. The small egg cracked with the force of a bomb. Mom stared at broken pieces from a life she had long ago. Her face turned white, every freckle showing, and my fists clenched.

He staggered around waving a tire iron in the air; muscled from working a jackhammer for the city all his sorry life and ugly drunk. Flowers flew off the table with sprays of water and shattered glass. Cursing, he went after Mom. This time I was ready. I wrestled it out of his filthy hands and hit him good. He lay torn up, didn't move, blood everywhere on Mom's clean kitchen floor. I stood there looking down at my father and thought how hard it was going to be for Mom to get the blood up. And how come he was the worst father in the world scaring all of us, hurting Mom and me. I breathed too fast and almost threw up. We were safe now because I'd done this terrible thing and I didn't know how I could live with it.

Mom's thick auburn hair came loose from her bun and she looked so pretty bending over him, a finger pressed to his neck as if she was a cop. On tiptoes, she pulled the ceiling fan chain and her sleeve rolled back. Black and blue marks covered her arm. I counted them. Mom had a lot more than I did. The breeze felt good. Then she wiped my fingerprints off the tire iron and replaced them with hers.

RECONSTRUCTING CHARLIE

I watched Mom change from quiet refined Liz Costigan to someone I didn't know.

"No more sweltering in my house," she said. She reached in his pants like a pickpocket and came up with a handful of dollars and coins. Handing me the money, Mom said, "I guess he drank the rest of his pay. Sorry it's not more. Let's get you packed."

She was in charge, this new mother, and I didn't question her. Icy cold inside myself, Mom dragged me along to my bedroom. I kept looking back expecting him to come after us.

"Reach up high on the top shelf, Charlie. Bring the suitcase down."

Mom's hands caressed the leather case I'd never seen.

"I packed my clothes and ran away sixteen years ago," she said. "I was wild, out-of-control."

"Were you ever sorry, Mom?"

"I have you and Jimmy, and my little girls. Take a shower. I have things to do." She pushed me toward the hall.

I heard Mom opening and closing drawers, knew she'd be too busy to worry about me for a while and crept back to the bloody mess to make sure he really was dead. His dark eyes had turned to an empty stare. Shivering, I ran for the bathroom. Even a hot shower couldn't warm me and blood refused to wash off. Words spun around in my head. 'Out, out, damned spot.' I scrubbed 'til it hurt. *Lady Macbeth, that's me.*

Wrapped in a towel, I watched Mom empty my clothes into her suitcase. I couldn't move. He's dead in the house and she packed my clothes for what? Mom added a dress hanging at the back of the closet, folded and placed it on top. The sound of the zipper closing on the suitcase startled me into action. I pried up the board in the closet, removed my money, and secured it into a money belt I'd bought in a second hand shop. Mom nodded approval.

"Wear this," she said, handing me jeans and a long sleeved tee shirt. I dug some underwear out of the suitcase and dressed. "Take a windbreaker. Air conditioning on the bus."

Unfastening a gold locket on a long chain she wore around her neck, she said, "Hold up your hair, my girl."

We stood face to face, her hazel eyes looking into mine. I heard a tiny click when the clasp was in place around my neck. She kissed the locket and let it slide under my shirt.

"What's in the locket, Mom?"

"Two sisters, my dear Charlie. One wise. One foolish." Mom smiled the saddest smile. She held my face in both hands. "Yes, I have a sister, your aunt Eleanor. Now listen hard. Money and education. Most important. And one more thing, precious girl, don't let boys catch your scent. Keep clean. That's something I forgot."

Scared and bewildered, I wasn't used to her making fast decisions. Any decisions.

"I'll call the police after you're gone. It was self-defense. There are hospital records of abuse for years. The Union will take financial care of us. Your job is to make a new life. Catch a bus to Chicago. My sister is there."

She pulled a box out from a drawer in my small desk and opened it. Fancy stationery paper, the old fashioned kind with the scent of flowers. Taking a deep breath, mom wrote in her perfect handwriting. I always believed mom had a lot of secrets. Now I got a peek at some just before I was leaving. Not fair and I felt like my little sisters when they stamped their feet against the world. I didn't want to leave. She tucked two sheets of paper in a matching envelope and added an address.

"Don't lose this, Charlie. It's your passport to a new life."

I couldn't speak. Somehow words got stuck in my throat so I read the name Mom had written. Mrs. Stuart Alfred. I unzipped a side pocket on my backpack and placed the envelope in with care.

"Don't let her turn you away. She's my older sister. She hated your father."

I never saw her cry before and when tears fell, she brushed them away.

Panic set in. "What if she's not there?"

"She'll be there, same as always. I've kept in touch with her. Not often. Just enough."

So sure of herself, this new mother.

"Charlie," Mom looked in my eyes so deep as if she was taking a picture, "don't call. I'll call you when I have something to say. Now hurry. It's not too late to catch the bus."

Mom hugged me and I ran.

RECONSTRUCTING CHARLIE

Fifteen years old traveling alone for the first time. First thing I did was head for the restroom. Not too many people in the bus terminal. A sign said the bus to Chicago would leave in a half hour. Midnight. Locking the stall, I counted money. My money. Didn't come to much. Two hundred twenty three dollars and forty two cents. Bus ticket, snack, cab ride to Lake Shore Drive, wherever that was. Sounded beautiful.

I tucked long hair inherited from my mother under an old slouch hat from the second hand shop; took out what might cover the ticket and food when the bus stopped and I was ready. I'd play this new life like a game of chess, think moves ahead. Okay. When I got to Chicago, I'd change into mom's dress and clean up to make a nice impression on Aunt Eleanor and Uncle Stuart.

But what if they hate me and slam the door in my face? Not possible, kid. You're dynamite. Ever since you started school, teachers talked about you when they didn't know you were listening. Smart, they said. Lots of potential.

Walking tough, I stepped close to the ticket window, lowered my voice and asked for a one way ticket to Chicago. The man behind the glass didn't look up when he said 'have a good trip, son.' A ticket came through the bottom of the cage after I paid less than expected. An express bus. I could be cleaned up and on Lake Shore Drive by ten in the morning. The conductor called for all aboard. I climbed on, took a seat near the front and kept my gear at hand, pleased no one tried to sit next to me, the tough kid in the second seat. I munched on a granola bar and drank a bottle of milk. Dinner.

I felt like a thief opening mom's letter to her sister but couldn't resist. Careful, so careful not to tear the envelope, I found mom hadn't sealed it. She knew me so well.

Dear Eleanor,

Did you ever wonder about the hang-up phone calls over the years? It was me, embarrassed to say hello and wanting to hear your voice. Sixteen years have gone by since your foolish sister ran away. I've paid for it dearly. I am so sorry I didn't listen to you and Stuart. And then it was too late. I was pregnant with the young woman standing before you and too humiliated to ask for your counsel.

Please embrace her, Eleanor, and make her your own. I cannot provide proper care for this gifted and brave daughter. She's smart and clever like her aunt and ambitious. You won't be disappointed. I've tried and succeeded in teaching her everything you taught me. She is a better student than I was.

My husband is dead and now my family and I will be fine. Charlotte is the one I can't do justice for. She's called Charlie and it suits her.

I send my love to you and Stuart and hope we meet again.

Your sister,

Elizabeth

I folded the letter and returned it to the envelope. Were the tear stains Mom's or mine?

I wasn't into prayer much but this seemed like a good time for a simple one. Closing my eyes, I prayed to God for a decent life for my family. When I opened my eyes, an image of Dad lying on the floor appeared in front of me. I shuddered.

Staring into the night, lights flashing by, I wondered how everything got out of control. It wasn't my fault. A baby is born, parents take care. If I was ever a parent, that's what I'd do. I'd protect my kids and love. . .

No one to share the story with. Not ever. A lonely road ahead with secrets.

My thoughts turned to a secret place deep inside my head where I buried what had happened tonight.

A few tears leaked out. I shook my head. A better image surfaced. The plan for Charlie Costigan. To skyrocket as high as I could fly.

Chicago.

First off the bus with my gear, first to find the restroom sign. I barreled through a crowd bent on being first in, first out. Scared and excited by strangers and noise levels never heard before, I used every bit of strength like a linebacker breaking through. Ladies gave me a sharp look when I came in and laughed when my hat tumbled to the floor. My hair was a mess. I shook my head hard, ran fingers through for a quick fix and checked in the mirror. Not good enough for Aunt and Uncle.

Dragging my stuff into the nearest stall, I locked the door and rummaged through Mom's suitcase. Sure enough, she'd tucked her favorite pearl comb and brush set in a side pocket plus some wipe-ups and a deodorant. I whispered thanks and got busy. Off came old jeans and the shirt I'd traveled in. I sniffed my pits. Not too gross. I washed up in the sink, slipped into the long sleeved dress, and brushed the hell out of my hair until it shone. My sneakers didn't make a fashion statement but they were all I had. I did a twirl around. Charlie Costigan, you don't exactly look like the cover of Vogue. I did a double take. I was the image of Mom.

A woman passed by and said, "Nice dress. Vintage?"

"Uh, yes. Thanks."

Ladylike, I made my way to an information booth in the gigantic building where there were buses and trains and too many signs.

"How do I get to Lake Shore Drive?" I said.

"Cab's your best bet, Miss. Out in front."

I hurried into the morning heat of Chicago. Culture shock. Tallest buildings. Crowds of people rushing like disturbed ant colonies. Ten in the morning. Too early to knock on their door? A line of taxi cabs waited. I hurried over like a country bumpkin but I had to be smart. Didn't want to be taken advantage of by city smart drivers.

Knocking politely on the cab door, I asked the driver if he knew where Lake Shore Drive was. When he barked, "Get in," I walked away. No one's going to talk to me like that. I searched for a friendly face and spotted a cop, an older guy in uniform talking with a younger man, plain clothes. He had the look. I could smell them. Mom always said, when in doubt, ask a cop. Time to put a forlorn expression on my face and I approached.

"Excuse me," I drawled, "I'm trying to get to my aunt. She works at a house on Lake Shore Drive and everyone here is so nasty. Is there some safe means of transportation I can take?" I blinked my eyes, just like Mom's, and tried to look dumb and sweet. A big stretch for me.

They looked me up and down, took in my present state and decided to help. Chicago--a wonderful town. The younger one said, "I live on the near north side. I can give you a lift. Have a drink, an iced tea or something and come back. Patrick Donnelly at your service, Miss." He offered his hand. I shook it, careful not to squeeze too hard, delicate little flower me. His friend nodded as if to say good work, Pat.

"Charlie Costigan," I dimpled back.

16

Chicago, do you hear my name?

I passed a kiosk where cold drinks were sold and took a drink from a water fountain.

Fifteen minutes later, I sat beside a nice looking guy in a tan Ford Taurus, fully equipped with cop stuff. Not bad for starters. He maneuvered fast and smooth through heavy traffic, horns blaring. He didn't pay attention but I did and then he turned a corner. For me, a world opened to reveal my future; a place I'd bring my family to someday. Patrick drove down the most beautiful wide street I'd ever seen. Of course, I had never been anywhere outside of the mean streets of the town I planned to forget but this was something out of a dream.

Glancing at me, Patrick Donnelly grinned. "This is called the Magnificent Mile. Michigan Avenue. On your right is the Art Institute with the lion statues. All the famous shops are here both sides of the avenue, and see the Sears Tower?" He pointed to the right. "Lake Michigan is just on the other side of all the buildings. Beaches, the zoo. Too bad it's so early. We could stop for a drink before I drop you off." He gave me a sideways look. "Or maybe tonight?"

I said, "I'm fifteen."

His face was impassive although I caught a glimpse of a muscle twitch in his jaw.

"Call me when you're eighteen." We laughed.

I saw a sign. Lake Shore Drive. No way was I going to give him the right address.

When the numbers got close, I said, "Here we are. My aunt told me to go around to the back entrance. I can't wait to see her."

The door handle didn't open. Cop car. I hid the panic rising in me and hoped for the best.

"Sorry. I always lock it from my side."

Double click and I was out breathing free, backpack and suitcase in hand. "Thanks so much, Patrick. This was a big help."

Leaning out the window, his strong hand grasped mine and just for a minute, I thought he'd pull me close. I didn't want anyone to do that. Not now, maybe not ever. But all the nice guy did was hand me a card.

"Charlie, if you ever need a friend, call me. I mean it. Good luck."

RECONSTRUCTING CHARLIE

I watched him drive away before I walked a few more blocks to the front door of a tall old building that looked like a picture come to life.

Chapter 2

My reflection in the spotless glass door greeted me. This is what they'd see when the door opened. I tried out a few smiles, mouthed some hello's I should have rehearsed on the bus. All those hours and I was down to the wire. After smoothing unruly hair and wishing for a band to put up a pony tail, I took a few deep breaths.

Mom's letter in hand, I rang and chimes echoed somewhere in the house. A polished brass knocker gleamed center door. A man dressed in a dark suit opened the door. Uncle Stuart?

"Yes?" he said. A man of few words.

"I'm Elizabeth's daughter."

A woman who looked familiar, an older version of Mom and much better-dressed, walked down a curved staircase and moved like she floated on a cloud toward me. She stopped and cried out.

"Elizabeth." Arms outstretched, she embraced me.

Mistaken identity. I thought she looked like Mom and she believed I was her sister. Just for a moment. We both cried. Just for a moment.

With hands so soft, they'd never washed a dish, she held me at arm's length.

"You are Elizabeth's daughter."

"Yes."

"Edgar, please take her bags upstairs to the first guest room. Thank you."

Not Uncle Stuart.

My Aunt Eleanor led the way to what she called the drawing room.

"Did you travel by bus to come here?"

"Yes."

"From?"

"Minnesota."

"Minnesota. Hmm. You traveled all night and must be hungry."

She lifted a small silver bell and shook it. Like magic, Edgar appeared.

"This is my niece, Edgar."

His expression didn't change as if nieces showed up every day.

"Please ask Mrs. Appleton to prepare a hearty breakfast as soon as possible. Thank you."

I handed Mom's letter to my aunt. My aunt. I loved the words. They rolled around in my mouth as I digested the sweet taste of family who might be interested in me.

Glasses on a gold chain were perched on her slender nose and she read. Finally, she looked at me.

"You are the image of your mother and the dress you're wearing is one I purchased for her a long time ago." Aunt Eleanor shook her head. "Well, my dear Charlie, whatever in the world is my husband going to think about this." She leaned toward me. "And watch his face when he sees you." Her hazel eyes sparkled. "Stuart was quite taken with my baby sister."

Taken. I wondered what that meant. Too soon to ask, I decided.

Soon Edgar arrived with the requested breakfast. We sat in a cozy morning room with hanging spider plants and wicker furniture. Scrambled eggs, crisp bacon, silver dollar pancakes, iced tea in tall crystal tumblers topped with lemon in little mesh caps. I'd have to behave myself in this house, if they let me stay. *Please let me stay.*

"Mrs. Appleton has been with us for many years. She's a marvelous chef so please eat, dear girl, while I tell you a story."

My silver fork, poised midway to my salivating mouth with half a pancake ready to be devoured, waited.

My elegant aunt spoke in a voice like a movie star. Her eyes crinkled with good humor.

"Go on. Eat and listen." She sipped iced tea. "Your mother was a bit of a dickens as a toddler."

I swallowed a half pancake, almost choked and said, "Dickens like the children in Charles Dickens stories?" Mom —a wild child as a baby; in her blood and maybe in mine? I shivered deep inside.

"Yes. She marched to a different beat, my baby sister. We went through nannies often. Our mother had no patience." Seeing my surprise at the words 'our mother', she chuckled. "Yes, you had a Grandmama. Your mother's behavior finally did her in. She's gone on beyond us now. Back to little Elizabeth. I loved her to pieces but I'm ten years older and she was like a toy."

She stopped telling the story and I knew Aunt Eleanor wanted me to finish breakfast so I dug in.

"When I was fifteen and Elizabeth was five, I found it necessary to lock my bedroom door. Her clever fingers found ways into my drawers, jewelry box, make-up supplies, nothing was sacred."

My aunt leaned forward in the intimate way she'd done before.

"One day I brought my beau home, the house so quiet I assumed no one was home. We'd have some privacy. Hormones, you know." A becoming blush rose in her cheeks. She glanced in my direction for understanding.

No nod from me because I never intended to do what she described. Never. I'd taken a private vow of celibacy and guys with a hard on could go fuck themselves.

"And I forgot to lock the door. We were carrying on as young people do when we heard giggling right behind us. We both looked up to find little Elizabeth waving my lingerie around and dancing."

She looked serious and I wanted to crack up.

"Then what happened?"

"Even as a teen, my beau appreciated the humor and I told you he was always taken with your mother."

Taken with my mother? What did that mean?

"You're saying the boyfriend was, is Uncle Stuart?"

Her laugh sounded like the silver bell she used to summon Edgar.

"Well, of course. It was the year of my coming out and Stuart said it was unseemly. And we never indulged again until we married five years later."

"Coming out?"

"Yes, dear. That's another story."

After the delicious meal where I remembered to keep my left hand in my lap--no elbows on the table, a meal complete with an inside story of mom, more than I wanted to know about my aunt and uncle, she showed me to a guest room on the second floor and said I should make myself at home.

"There are fresh towels and everything you might need. Stuart will be home before long."

She left, footsteps muffled by thick carpet; her scent lingered, something light and sweet.

"Thank you," I said, and looked around. Breathtaking. Everything so perfect, matched, luxurious. And a four poster bed. I tried it out, bounced a few times and stretched out. King size. The past twenty four hours hit me. Did the cops believe Mom or were they searching for me? Running away like a coward, leaving Mom and the kids. What a piece of shit I am. If I cried and screamed, everything Mom wanted for me would end. Rolling over on the big bed with silky sheets, I pressed my face down and stifled all feelings. Then I ran to the bathroom.

Carefully, I unbuttoned my dress and found a hanger. Didn't want to wrinkle it. Too late, I heard a knock on the door and suddenly my aunt was in the doorway of the bathroom. Me in a bra and panties and she had a hand over her mouth as she saw my bruises—on my back and arms.

"Oh, Charlie."

Embarrassed, I covered up with a towel. "I heal fast, Aunt Eleanor. In two weeks they'll be gone and no one will ever hurt me again. Really, I'll be okay."

"Oh, Charlie."

She appeared to be stricken by the sight and then careful not to touch the bruises, Aunt Eleanor reached for my necklace. It lay forgotten against my chest. She opened the locket studying both pictures. I heard Mom's voice saying, "Two sisters, one wise—one foolish." And a flood of tears released from me. *Tough Charlie Costigan. Always in control.* She held me in her arms the way I'd held Mom a million times. My aunt was older and felt kind of fragile but I bet she had a core of steel.

I repeated, "I'll be okay."

"Yes you will. I'll make sure of it."

Backing away with tears in her eyes, my aunt left, her silk dress spotted with my guilt and shame.

Chapter 3

Fresh from the shower, hair clean from products I'd read about in magazines, I was almost ready to meet my uncle. Aunt Eleanor had been horrified to find I had no other shoes but my sneakers and said she'd remedy the situation either this afternoon or the following day. "Remedy the situation." What a neat way of speaking. I planned to learn a lot from this wonderful aunt of mine.

Manly voices downstairs. I 'd been told to stay in my room, no hardship since books filled shelves and I got right back into Anna Karenina. What an idiot to end up on the tracks but the writing was magical. Crime and Punishment called to me. I pushed it in a corner.

The light voice of Aunt Eleanor floated up the stairs. She'd said Stuart needed a drink when he arrived home. The thought of alcohol made me sick. I prayed he wasn't like Dad. Nothing new until the drink, she'd said, some cashews, and a few kisses. Yes, she confided in me, the interloper in their peaceful life. Maybe, since she hadn't talked about kids of her own, Aunt Eleanor missed the friendship of a young woman. Mom always had me, deep thinker, Charlie.

A tap at the door. "Your presence is requested in the drawing room, Miss," Edgar's deep voice echoed in me.

Dress smoothed, hair okay, I tried not to gallop down the stairs. Shoulders back, head erect the way Miss Betty in gym class taught years before, I entered and offered a shy smile I'd practiced while applying a little make-up.

Uncle Stuart rose to his feet. About five feet ten, kind of overweight—not too much, he looked nice. A sparkle in his eye, not scary like Dad and so many boys in school and men on the streets, but curious and friendly. He liked what he saw. I knew it from experience.

"Yes, you are the image of your mother. How is she? Well, I hope?"

RECONSTRUCTING CHARLIE

"Better now, thank you."

"Well, let us dine and discuss our situation after dinner."

He offered one arm to me and one to my aunt and we walked to yet another room called the dining room. Back home we ate all our meals in the kitchen.

A shakiness threatened entering the beauty of a real dining room. I called on every bit of strength from all the years growing up and surviving Dad to the moment I arrived at this doorstep with blood barely washed off my hands.

When Edgar offered to pour wine in my glass, I said, "No, thank you. Water will be fine." And dinner began.

To the left of my plate were a lot of forks. *Why?* Knives and a bunch of spoons on the right. No wonder Aunt Eleanor never did dishes. Too much and what for? It made no sense. Not to me. I shut my mouth and watched.

Another man, younger, dressed in a white jacket and tie came to each of us with soup. He ladled it from a big bowl. A signal from my aunt showed me the right spoon to use. She saved my butt from making an error during my first dinner. The soup was red, cold, and not bad with bits of shrimp in it. The whole meal unfolded like a stage play at school, attention to every detail, quiet conversation with my aunt asking Uncle Stuart about his day in court and his polite answer to her every question, soft music in the background. Me, the observer from a dysfunctional family, where everyone ate with one fork, knife, and spoon, burped and ran, dropped into this atmosphere of peace and . . .*what's a good word, c'mon, Charlie, you're smart. . .*gentility. *Yes. Listen and soak it up like a sponge.*

Relieved when dinner ended, almost sure I wouldn't be asked to do the dishes, Uncle Stuart said, "Let's relax in my study where we shall discuss the situation, ladies."

The shivers began inside Mom's dress as I followed my new-found family to another part of the big house. Lots of controlled breathing on my part, step by step. Entering the dark wood paneled room, the smell of lemon furniture polish almost knocked me over. A heavy hand with the spray bottle made the wood shine. Books lined floor to ceiling shelves with a ladder attached to reach everywhere like some fancy library. My fingers itched to climb the ladder, explore the books. His study, he'd said. What kind of business? I wondered and then the mystery cleared. Shelves of law books. Must be a lawyer. Charlie, super sleuth.

We sat in buttery soft leather chairs, the three of us in a semi-circle.

Clearing his throat, Uncle Stuart began. "Your aunt and I want to ask a few questions, not to embarrass you but rather to find out who you are. Have you any ideas about what you want for your future, do you have an interest in sports, music, and so forth." Sitting back, hands folded across his chest, he waited. His face changed. He looked kind of like the guys dad played poker with when they didn't want anyone to know about the cards they held. Maybe a lawyer face.

"Take your time, Charlie. Think it over. Would you like a chocolate?" My aunt gestured to a plate on the nearby table. "Chocolate helps me think."

If I had a chocolate--I wanted all of them—I'd throw up. Too nervous.

"I'll answer your questions in order as best I can. I want to earn a lot of money and I know I can do it. Business. Some kind of business. I'll learn as I go along in school. I'm very smart as you'll find out. Mom said I'm a lot like Aunt Eleanor. I always worked after school so there wasn't time for sports but every team wanted me because they knew how fast and strong I am. Music, again I worked all the time to help out at home, I never learned an instrument. It's never too late to learn. I'm fifteen and I have a clear two octave singing voice. Alto. As for, and so forth, one way or the other, I'm going to college and become somebody."

Now I reached for a dark chocolate and bit into the best taste ever. Hmm. A lot like Mrs. Kowalski's fudge store where she always gave me free tastes 'cause I shoveled the snow in front of her shop.

Well, I told the truth. Good thing he didn't ask about dear old Dad.

Gesturing to the plate of chocolates, Uncle Stuart's voice you didn't want to cross said, "I'll have one of those."

"But Stuart, you never eat chocolate."

"I feel the need."

Silence in the room as the rich--how I love that word--smell of chocolate battled lemon polish and won.

Settling back, Uncle patted his jacket for something. In awe, I watched my aunt lean over, a white handkerchief in her graceful hand, and dab at a dark tell-tale spot at the corner of his mouth.

RECONSTRUCTING CHARLIE

This is what marriage must be all about. Poor Mom missed the boat.

Uncle Stuart had more questions. "Your name is Charlotte and I understand from your mother's letter you prefer Charlie. Correct?"

"Yes."

"You didn't bring transcripts from high school."

"No, I didn't." I almost said, no sir, Mom told me to run. "I test well under pressure." Almost said, no sweat, pressure's my middle name.

I slid a glance over to Aunt Eleanor. She nodded as if everything was going the way she planned. *I'm a planner like her.*

"Eleanor and I have discussed a few options regarding you. One is a private girl's school, nearby, highest academic standards, excellent music, art, and a sports program. If you qualify and if you like it. The other is a fine public school. Monday, I could make some calls and set up testing. See where you'd fit in. One positive is that the school year is just beginning. It will be difficult transferring at your age."

Uncle, if you think this is difficult, you don't know nothin'. Inside I cringed at the word. Difficult is when I spent every day protecting my family from a father who beat our mother and sometimes me. Difficult is when I got my period and boobs started to pop and dad had the look in his eyes when he pushed against me with ideas a father should never have for a daughter.

The gentle voice of my aunt said, "What do you think of these possibilities, Charlie?"

I gave them the grateful smile I thought they expected. "I don't want to cost you a bunch of money. Private school sounds expensive. How about if I take the tests, see what happens, and then we can all decide what's best?"

They beamed; we toasted with one more piece of chocolate, and the dearest couple in the whole world said it was time for bed. A kiss on the cheek from my new family and off to sleep. Exhausted, I stretched out under silky sheets after thanking God for kindness shown to me. I prayed Mom and the kids were okay and fell asleep.

Sometime during the night, the first nightmare came starring dear old Dad, James Costigan. The sickening thud of a tire iron when I hit him. Blank eyes, a pool of blood, Mom's bruised arm turning on the ceiling fan. Click, click. Scenes rolled past like a movie. Frozen in place, I didn't move until the part where Mom said, "Run."

Then I ran to the beautiful bathroom and threw up.

'Begin again, Costigan' were my last thoughts before sleep. Tomorrow Aunt Eleanor and I were going shopping.

Chapter 4

Before leaving on the shopping expedition, in Aunt Eleanor's words, she asked if we might look through my clothes and see what I needed. All my stuff was clean, wearable by small town standards and I wasn't ashamed of what Mom had packed. I made small piles of underwear, three shirts, a couple pair of jeans, socks, and a sweater. Laid them out on the bed. They were lost on the king size. The way I felt. Not much to look at but it was mine. Mom's brush and comb lay next to the pile.

A knock at the door and she came in, dressed to shop. Pretty in a white sweater set with pearls, a print silk skirt and white pumps, the picture of a summer garden. By comparison, I'd look like a lumberjack next to her.

"Hmm. You packed in a hurry, didn't you, dear?" Picking up Mom's brush and comb, she smiled. "I gave this set to her when she was quite young. This is her way of saying hello to me."

Together, we said, "Maybe wear the dress, for now." Laughing, we left my meager belongings behind.

Robert drove the limousine to Michigan Avenue. He doubled as wait staff/chauffeur. I learned later he was hired to help Edgar during an illness and stayed on.

"There's a nice shop one of my dear friend goes to with her daughter. It's on the Magnificent Mile not too far from here. Robert knows where. They have the latest in teenage fashions from shoes up." She patted my hand. "Let's have some fun, Charlie. Uncle Stuart wants you to have the best."

Teenage fashions. I never had much time to think about fashion or teenage. Once in a while I'd find a Seventeen Magazine or some other rag with clothes way over my head. Who'd a thunk it? Charlie Costigan in a limousine shopping.

"Do they have dressing rooms?"

"You'll have all the time and privacy you need. Don't worry."

RECONSTRUCTING CHARLIE

It was ten o'clock, the shop had just opened and we were first in. Aunt Eleanor requested Corrine as salesperson and a woman hurried out. They exchanged greetings, I was introduced and Corrine circled me as if she were looking for clues.

"Beauty hiding in the vintage dress and old sneakers. We do a makeover, yes?"

"Yes," Aunt Eleanor said.

We'll see, I thought.

"What are the latest fall fashions? My niece will be going to high school here. She's fifteen."

"Leggings with slouch socks and white Keds are very popular. Girls are wearing long loose sweaters or sweatshirts over them. Form fitting tee shirts short in length showing a hint of bare midriff with wide leg blue jeans." As Corinne spoke, her busy hands pulled clothes from racks.

I didn't have a clue about leggings and slouch socks but when she said bare midriff, I thought—get me out of here.

"The androgynous look is popular although it would be a shame to hide such beauty in a shapeless form. Body shirts are in. Layered look. Waffle undershirt with plaid flannel worn over. Short skirts and long jackets."

Yeah, androgynous. That's for me. Body shirts are out.

Another salesperson came over to help carry the mountain of clothes to a dressing room the size of a bedroom back home. Two comfortable chairs, fashion magazines and a small table. Aunt Eleanor looked wistful so I invited her in. She'd already seen my bruised body.

"Thank you, Corinne. We'd like some privacy now. I'll call for assistance, if needed," she said to the eager woman.

"Well, let's see what works for you, Charlie. If you need my opinion or help, I'm here." She settled in a chair. I heard the rustle of paper as she opened a magazine. An angel.

Where to begin. Mom's dress unbuttoned, I hung it up and slipped into a form fitting tee shirt exposing my belly button and higher. My little sisters could fit in it. NO! Carefully, I folded the shirt and tried a long sleeved beige shirt in the softest waffle pattern. Perfect. Then I sat and pulled on black leggings. Stretchy and felt great. Corinne said slouch socks went over them. Okay. I pulled on the socks. Way cool. My legs were definitely amazing. I needed something to cover my ass. A long forest green sweater did the job. She'd also placed a short skirt in the pile. For kicks, I stepped into the plaid skirt and zipped it.

Oh my god! I didn't recognize myself.

Aunt Eleanor held up a page from the magazine showing a model dressed a lot like me.

"Very nice, Charlie. Try on some more. Put your selections on the side. By the way, what size do you wear?"

Size? Never thought about size. I looked for a tag. "2." I looked at another tag. "1."

"Hmm." She went back to the magazine, a grin on her face.

Laden with packages, Robert packed the trunk of the limousine and resumed waiting while we had lunch and discussed the adventures of shopping, new to me and fun for my aunt. She was greeted with courtesy at a cool restaurant, ushered in as if we were royalty. I was introduced once again as her niece come to live with them, to attend school. My chest tightened to see her pleasure. I vowed to give back, to make these good people proud of me.

"Charlie, Stuart and I were never blessed with children. It's a long story and in the past but now you're here with us. Somehow, fate in the name of Elizabeth, brought you to our door. We talked about you far into the night last night." Leaning toward me, my aunt said, "I can't replace your mother but I want you to know you can trust me, confide in me. Don't ever feel alone. Not ever."

Her words gave me hope. The waiter came and I ate my first shrimp salad. Yum. We went home.

Chapter 5

Taking the stairs two at a time, I hurried to my room with bags of clothes slapping against my legs. Aunt Eleanor's laughter carried from the first floor. I heard her say, "Stuart, she's delightful, exuberant. . ." and somewhere in the big house, a door closed.

Alone to unwrap, hang up, maybe try on again, fold and put in drawers, my new clothes. Mine. With care, I removed new blue jeans, a white tee shirt in a bigger size so my midriff didn't show, a jean jacket and white socks. Ked sneakers would take some getting used to, so white and neat. There I stood in a new bra and silky cotton blend panties with lace trim. What a difference from the washed a million times underwear I brought with me.

Charlie, I said to the girl in the full length mirror, you look pretty damn good. Tall and kind of skinny but okay. I did a little dance and went to work. After the room looked in order, I needed a run to check out the neighborhood. I dressed in shorts, struggled into a sports bra to harness the boob jiggle and pulled over an old shirt. The new running shoes held my feet in all the right places. I hoped my family wouldn't mind me going out for a while.

Aunt Eleanor met me on the stairs, a smile on her face.

She said, "The phone rang before and when I said hello and no one answered, I knew it was your mother. Before she could hang up, I said, Charlie's here, Elizabeth. She's safe and we love her already. Don't worry. Then I heard the hang up click."

Touching my hand, she said, "I'm happy she called and that I had the good sense to speak."

I grabbed the railing and squeezed so hard my knuckles cracked. Filled with sadness and regret, I wanted to cry. Mom and the kids almost a thousand miles away and I'm in luxury.

My dear aunt's voice came from far away. "Be careful when you run. Traffic can be heavy on Saturday. Cross over the street and run north. You'll see parks along the way. We dine at seven."

"Okay." My footsteps were heavy on the stairs, the light happy feeling I had a few minutes before now gone.

Slow pace first, then I picked it up and pounded the sidewalk until I came to a park with a running path. Better. The hot day brought out lots of runners, bikers, people pushing baby strollers. Had to dodge to keep a decent pace. Sipped water from my new bottle. New. Everything about me new. Even my life. I checked my watch, almost four. How did it get so late? Ran my ass off. Wish I'd left a trail of bread crumbs to find my way home.

Home. The word took on new meaning. Dripping wet, I rang the bell. Edgar took one look at me, put a finger to his tight lips and beckoned me in to run upstairs. His message--Be quiet.

What to do with laundry piling up? Maybe the washing machine and dryer were in the basement. I wanted to explore the house, take a tour. Better ask Aunt Eleanor. Ask Edgar about laundry. Hanging wet clothes over the shower door, I dressed for the next family gathering and listened to the house. Except for classical music coming from somewhere, quiet. Never heard quiet before. Back home, three younger kids made life noisy. Mom and I always knew the fear Dad brought. Fear had a sound of its own.

At seven, demons gone, I waited for the dinner call.

We entered the pretty room where I'd had breakfast yesterday. Just yesterday when I arrived in Mom's old dress? Yellow birds on little swings sang in wire cages, spider plants hung from the beamed ceiling. They called it the garden room. I loved the outdoor feeling, the hemp carpet. A bouquet of Black eyed Susie's arranged just right in a glass vase on the table.

I stopped short and couldn't move. All of a sudden an image of Mom picking the same flowers from her small garden to make the table look nice for Dad escaped from the locked place in my head. *His arm shot out, glass shattered and petals flew up and off the table; water dripped across the table, drip, drip hitting the linoleum. I shivered.*

Uncle Stuart broke the spell. "Of all the rooms, this is my favorite. We like Saturday dinners in here when we aren't entertaining."

"It's so nice, like eating outside." *Clever conversationalist, Charlie. You can do better.*

A buffet set up on a side board with do-it-yourself service felt right for me. I took over as waitress, a job I'd had many times, and they seemed to get a kick out of me taking their orders. Cold salads, shrimp cocktail, lobster bisque in fancy bowls. Filling their china plates, I pictured Mom opening dented cans of tuna, adding salad dressing and chopped eggs, a loaf of white bread on the counter. Some day. . .I promised.

The sideboard held a beautiful fruit plate someone in the kitchen cut up and an assortment of pastries. My uncle and aunt chuckled at the attention to detail as I unfolded napkins with a flourish and imitated every restaurant scene in movies. What a kick. We laughed a lot and they laughed harder when I offered to clear and do the dishes.

"No, darling girl," Aunt Eleanor said. "We have staff for those tasks. This was just so much fun."

An opportunity to ask about the laundry came right then. "I wonder where the laundry is. My clothes are piling up and I'm used to. . ."

"Nonsense, Charlie," Uncle Stuart said. "We have employees for everything. Your job is to go to school and achieve your goals."

"But what can I do for you, both of you? I feel useless."

They exchanged glances, rose in unison, took me by the arms and led me from the room. Eyes twinkling, they walked me toward the back of the house where I heard barking. Dogs? Where did they come from?

Unlatching the back door to the outside, Uncle Stuart said, "Follow me. I want you to meet your new job."

Barreling toward me in the sultry evening were two furry orange—no, apricot color—bundles of wriggling puppies, Australian Labradoodles, about three to five months old. Intelligent, almost shed free and perfect for anyone with asthma allergies. Maybe because Uncle Stuart always cleared his throat and had a kind of cough.

Thrilled beyond words, I lifted one hand palm up with the stay signal. They stayed. My index finger pointed to the ground. They sat. Kneeling beside them, we three gazed at each other, love at first sight. I touched the ground. They laid down paws under chins, black eyes alert. Again I raised my hand for them to stay.

Aunt Eleanor touched my back. I couldn't have strung two words together, so overcome by contact with dogs I didn't know lived here.

"Charlie, did you work with dogs back home?"

Swallowing the lump on my throat, I said, "Yes. I helped a trainer and walked a lot of dogs."

She said, "These are not ordinary dogs."

Verbatim, I reeled off a half page of information on this breed.

"Oh my," she said. "Stuart, I believe our girl has a photographic memory."

My aunt called me 'our girl.' I wanted to dance on rooftops, sing in tall trees, build a monument to them.

When Uncle Stuart gave me a quizzical look, I said, "Yes. It's my secret. Now you know."

He patted his chest with pride. "Well, it seems you are very much like your aunt. She has the same gift. It's our secret now. No one will know and this special talent will take you far." He gestured to the dogs. "These two will be your job. All right? You will feed and walk them, make sure they are well behaved. We'll go over the particulars later. Neither Robert or any of the staff understand about pets and we weren't sure what to do when we ordered them trained and house broken. Then you arrived and now our once quiet home is filled with a new energy." His eyes mirrored Aunt Eleanor's with the fateful coincidence. "They arrived this afternoon while you were out running."

I watched these dear people, who accepted me at face value, walk back to the house and I stayed outside to play with the dogs.

"Wait. What are their names?"

"The pedigree names won't be used. We're not planning to show them. Why don't you name them, Charlie?"

Click. Latch closed. We three were alone to figure it out. I checked their private parts. Hmm. One male, one female and with pedigrees. La-dee-fuckin'-dah.

I stroked their ears and said, "Someday I'll get a degree, a bunch of them. How about Lord and Lady? "They quivered with delight.

Uncle Stuart opened the door. "Church tomorrow. Ten o'clock." He paused. "You do go to church, don't you?" and waited for my answer.

Church. Say yes. "Yes."

Heartburn. That's what I experienced for the first time on what seemed like an endless trip to church. Breakfast did not want to digest. I gulped fresh air as soon as the limousine door opened, felt warmth from the sun touch my cheeks and said to myself, *"It's a different church."*

Aunt and Uncle introduced me to elegant people on the way up wide steps and then we entered the biggest church in the world with smiling faces all around. We sat way down in front, not where I wanted to be. Nailed to the pew, I spied a small gold marker. Stuart and Eleanor Alfred. *They own the pew and they know everyone in Chicago. And the best thing is they like me a lot. Thanks, Mom, for sending me here.*

When services ended and families lined up for communion, I stood, obedient, ready to conform. A small girl about eight years old broke away from someone and put her hand in mine. She turned her head way up to see me. Dressed in bridal white, I recognized ruffles repaired with a fine stitch, she wore a band of white flowers in dark red hair. So pretty. She whispered, *"Ready for first communion?"*

The front doors of the church banged open, dear old Dad staggered down the carpeted aisle. Cursing, he grabbed his first born daughter, me--the little girl, by the back of the white dress, ripped it open for all to see the secondhand petticoat.

I never went to church after that. . .until today. I'd begin again in my new life but I could never go to confession. I asked my aunt and uncle about the little girl in the white dress. They each shrugged and said they had not seen the child.

Maybe God gave me a warning to forget the past and move on.

Chapter 6

The Hamilton Academy. My eyes bugged out behind new sunglasses at the mansion with a campus. Three long low modern buildings separate from the main building formed a triangle. Tennis courts way over on one side, a huge track for runners. Eight in the morning and the place was hopping with sports. I was there to be tested. Uncle Stuart escorted me to the mansion.

"Mrs. Larimore is an old friend. When I called her yesterday, she agreed to see you this morning. You said you test well. Now's the time to prove it, my girl."

Oh Uncle, you told me this yesterday so you're the one who's nervous, not me. I'm okay.

"By the way, you look very fine this morning. You and Eleanor make a good shopping team."

"Thank you for everything, Uncle Stuart."

Dressed in a white shirt, the short skirt, long tailored jacket, black opaque tights and black shoes, I was a fashion statement. I also brought along a gym bag with running shoes and gear just in case. Robert would take Uncle Stuart to work and come back when I called him on my new portable phone. Whoopee-fuckin'-doo. I'll have to stop thinking with curse words. But not today.

Mrs. Larimore sat behind a large polished desk. She rushed from her chair right into my uncle's outstretched arms and planted a big kiss on his cheek. A really good old friend, I guessed.

"And this is your niece. Welcome to Hamilton Academy." She stood about five feet two in short heels and looked up at me with a tilt of her head. "Why, she's the image of Eleanor. What is your name?"

"Charlotte Costigan. I prefer to be called Charlie."

Bird-like, she gave me another tilt and a smile. "Ah yes." Turning to Uncle Stuart who watched over me like a father should, she said, "Charlie will be in good hands, Stuart. I'll call you later with test scores." Hand tucked firmly under his arm, she escorted him to the door.

RECONSTRUCTING CHARLIE

He turned and waved as if I had a journey to take and maybe I did. "Call Robert when you're ready to come home." The big door closed behind him and butterflies flew around my insides. Smoothing my hair and making a minor adjustment to my new headband for personal distraction, I waited.

"Follow me, Charlie. Let's get the testing over with. Then someone will show you around our campus."

I sat alone in a large room filled with, I did a quick scan, fifty desks. In front of me were four number two pencils all sharpened and lined up like soldiers at the ready. Several tests on different subjects in a small stack were handed to me by a girl named Sally. She said she was a proctor and test administrator.

"When the clock strikes eight thirty, begin," she said and disappeared.

Social Studies—Global and American, Algebra, some kind of multiple choice personality questionnaire, English Lit, Biology, Spanish. I finished in fifty five minutes. She returned at nine and found me drinking a bottle of water and eating an apple.

Examining each test, she said, "You didn't write an essay."

"Sorry, there wasn't any paper to write on. If you give me some, I can write one now. And a question, can I pick a topic or do you select one?"

Sally grinned. "No one ever asked and between you and me, usually it takes a couple of hours to finish the tests. I'll take you back to Mrs. Larimore now."

Relieved, butterflies gone, I walked along with her more confident now. Pretty sure I aced everything. Algebra not my favorite but needed. Calculators would come in handy. Basic Spanish but not too bad. Personality test? Multiple choice good if you had multiple personalities. Charlie, the Comedian.

"Back so soon?" Mrs. Larimore said when Sally knocked then entered, me trailing behind.

"She finished in less than an hour. I'll grade and report." Sally almost bowed out.

Again the head tilt and questioning look from the headmistress. "Well, Charlie, did you find the tests that easy or too difficult? Or will it all be revealed?"

I had to smile. An interesting woman like no one I'd ever met. "Yes, Mrs. Larimore. The results are what everyone wants. I hope I did well."

She left her important place behind the desk and sat next to me, a frown between her eyebrows. "The girls who attend Hamilton Academy are from privileged backgrounds. From what I understand, you grew up in a small town not far from Minneapolis in what we call a different social strata. Do you know what I'm talking about?"

Yeah, I got it. They're rich—I'm a dirt farmer, by comparison. I nodded.

"Your aunt and uncle are one hundred per cent behind you. Today you will see the public high school. I'm suggesting, privately, my girls who have never been denied anything, come here. Young women who may not understand someone as down to earth as you."

A knock at the door and Sally burst in. "Sorry, Mrs., but you've got to see this." She handed her my test scores.

Adjusting her glasses, the headmistress read and reread each page. Face flushed, she said, "Sally, make copies of everything and bring them right back."

"In all my years, I have never seen perfect scoring before." It was my turn to blush. I didn't. "Would you like to see the playing field, gymnasium, locker rooms, meet the coaches?" Checking a gold and diamond watch, she said, "It's almost time for mid-morning snack. Join the teams in the cafeteria and I will personally introduce you. Your uncle said you might be interested in track."

Sally ran in, papers in folders.

"May I see them?"

"Of course," Mrs. Larimore said.

I scanned the tests and nodded. "Are these mine to keep?"

"Well, yes. We have copies. Well done, Charlie. Now about the cafeteria?"

I stood up tall in my fashion perfect outfit, perfect test scores in hand and said, "Thank you, Mrs. Larimore. I'm going to call Robert for a ride home to talk this over with my family.

Chapter 7

Uncle Stuart waited at the open door, a grin on his usual poker face. He said, "You aced the tests and had that bitch eating out of your hands."

"Really Stuart, watch your language."

Fuckin' A, I thought, and tried to look innocent. "I've heard a lot worse, Aunt Eleanor."

"Have a snack and we'll go over to the high school. I believe George Adams will accept these scores and make room for you there. Your choice, Charlie. Always your choice," my proud uncle said. "Always remember, it's the choices you make in life that determine your future. By the way, did you walk the dogs, are they fed?"

"Yes to everything. Lord and Lady were good dogs last night."

"Lord and Lady?" he said.

"You told me to name them. With those impressive pedigrees, they deserve royal names, don't you agree?" Aunt Eleanor poured juice. "Stuart, I believe you've met your match in Charlie. Lord and Lady will do fine. Now eat some eggs and toast for protein and carbohydrates and drink orange and pomegranate juice. All good brain food. Then everyone please get on with your business and leave me to some peace."

Checking his watch, a smile on his broad face, "Twenty minutes, Charlie."

I ran upstairs to change. More casual. Tried on for the tenth time the boot cut jeans. They showed off my butt. Not happy about that. Dark green tee shirt and denim jacket. Keds. Hair brushed loose and shiny with the help of a shine spray. Comfortable and after a long check in the mirror from every angle, I approved. Yippee.

Chapter 8

High School. My stomach clenched. A different city, more money but underneath nicer clothes, I bet the guys were the same. Never had time for girlfriends, didn't know what to expect. Scared shitless. Admit it and get over yourself. You've got a job to do.

Uncle Stuart and I strode up the long path on a mission. For an older man, he kept a good pace. Together we climbed the wide concrete steps. He told me about his day; important meetings ahead but first he had to get his niece, dropped from the sky on his doorstep only three days before, settled. I filled in the 'dropped from the sky' and made him laugh.

Already sweat trickled down my pits to wet my nice tee shirt. Glad I'd worn the jacket to hide any stains and cover the slamming of my over-active heart, I swung my gym bag back and forth to establish an air of cool.

"Nervous?" Uncle Stuart said.

"You bet."

"No one would ever know."

"Good."

Snapping to attention, a guard at the wide main entrance said, "I.D. please." After checking Uncle's driver's license, he said, "Mr. Adams is waiting for you in his office."

Uncle smiled, waved a friendly greeting and we sailed through. I wondered if he planned to be a politician or maybe he had too much fun just being.

Football players, a herd of guys horsing around, emptied the gym at the same time we headed down the extra wide hall, so opposite from the small high school back home. Eleven in the morning and their sweat smelled strong after practice. X ray vision eyes burned through my new clothes or maybe I imagined it. One guy called out, "Good morning, Mr. Alfred." Nodding to him, uncle said, "Thomas Donnelly. Nice boy, focused and smart from a good family."

Everyone isn't bad. Everyone isn't bad. Everyone isn't. . .Uncle Stuart held a door open for me. We went in.

After the men did the man stuff, handshakes, how's the family and all and I sat like the sweet niece, principal George Adams, greeted me with a smile to put me at ease, I guessed. Uncle Stuart handed him the test folder and sat back. I scanned the walls for framed diplomas and trophies. Wow. He'd gone to Northwestern and earned a bunch of degrees. Impressive. He stood about five foot eleven, broad shoulders, maybe played football years ago and wrestled. His crooked nose gave him away.

A shuffle of papers and he finished reviewing my efforts. Leaning forward on his elbows, he said, "Your scores place you in junior year. Are there any sports you excel in?"

"I'm fast. I think track is my best bet." Heat rose in my cheeks. I'd never been on a team but I knew how to outrun rats in an alley, rats with two feet and four feet.

Pressing a button on his phone, Mr. Adams said, "Cora, get Betty Garrison on the line. Thanks."

He stood up. "Thanks for bringing your niece here, Stuart. We'll help the transition along."

I hugged my uncle. He slipped fifty dollars in my hand, for lunch or a down payment on a car, and said, "Call Robert when you're ready to come home."

And now I belonged to another new place, the first big step in education and moving forward with my plan. Randolph High School. A junior. Two years here and next, Northwestern University.

Dressed in running gear, a woman who'd spent a lot of time outside, burst into the office. "What's up, George. You're calling me in the middle of workout. I don't like that."

"Calm down, Betty. This is Charlie Costigan, Stuart Alfred's niece. You remember Mr. Alfred, don't you? He's the top lawyer in town, very influential. She's enrolling here and wants to try out for track, cross country, everything the team competes in."

She looked me up and down, shook her head, wiped sweat from her brow. "We've got just about all the girls. . ."

Mr. Adams said, "Betty."

That shut her up.

With a shake of her head, short brown hair flinging a few drops of sweat, she shrugged. "Follow me."

Nice to be wanted.

The principal called out, "Return to the office when you finish, Charlie."

We hurried down the hall and entered the women's locker room. "Sorry I was abrupt but I hate when he interferes with my workouts." She pointed to a locker. "Change and go through that door to the field. I'll watch for you."

Gone. No special treatment no matter who I'm related to.

Alone and glad of it, I changed fast in case anyone barged in. My bruises had faded but not enough. Gear stashed and safe with a new combination lock, I did a few stretches and ran out the door. Betty Garrison waved from a distance. I trotted over. A bunch of faces greeted me without smiles. What the hell did I expect? Me, the competition.

Exercises, stretches, sprints, great to be outside with no worry about making money. I put Mom and the kids out of my head for now and concentrated. My guidance counselor back home once told me sports were very important when you want to get in college. Sports, academics, service.

Sizing up the girls, I figured the blond lean muscular one, Lori, to be the alpha runner, top dog. Miss Garrison made it obvious this would be my tryout. She assigned a lane on the track to each of us and yelled go.

I ran with the fear of Dad chasing me, ran as I'd never run before and kept running and never heard the coach shouting my name, calling me back. I ran until she drove up next to me in a golf cart and said, "Stop. You made the team, Charlie." A bottle of water from her hand to mine, an offer to drive me back. Back? I turned around to see the school in the distance and woods ahead. I accepted the ride.

By the time Coach left me at the locker room, the place had emptied. Nothing left but some blotted lipstick tissues, perfumed air, water puddles on the floor, and wet towels in a heap. *Did they ever think about maintenance workers who picked up after them? Nah.*

Under the lukewarm shower, I soaped up fast, rinsed and got out. Used the last towel on a shelf to dry and thought about the question Coach asked me after my run. She wanted to know if I used the image of someone chasing me to get in the zone. I said, "No. I just love to run."

Big fat lie. I'd been running for my life all my fifteen years.

The football team and I crossed paths again in the wide hall. This time, I heard whistles and a few calls of, "Hey, Speedy." I didn't pay attention to them and kept a steady pace to the principal's office. *Later for you, sweaty guys. All you want is to get laid.* The name Donnelly came back to me. The cop who gave me a ride. Common name. Must be a million Donnelly's.

Mr. Adams welcomed me and this time he meant it. Handing me a class schedule for the first semester, plenty of time left for track, I noticed, he said, "Classes begin in two weeks. You'll need a physical. Text books are here." He gestured to a stack of books. "You can take these home today. Keep up with academics and sports and you'll be ready for college in two years. This may be premature, but have you thought about colleges?"

I pointed toward one of his framed diplomas. "Northwestern's my choice."

"Why?"

"It's a long story, Mr. Adams. But that's my goal."

I thanked him and under the weight of books and gym bag, staggered out to the front of the building. Time to call Robert for a ride home. I checked out the lawn so perfect golfers could putt on the mowed surface. There were flowerbeds full of marigolds, tall and short, petunias so pretty they made my heart hurt. Winding red brick paths crossed everywhere and old oak trees with gnarled roots reaching out for water lay on top of the grass. *Mom would love this. Maybe she went to school here.* Stunned with the thought, my secret grew too heavy. Dropping my burdens, I sat on a stone bench to take a deep breath.

The black limousine pulled up. Robert to the rescue. He opened the door and tilted his head. I gathered myself and my stuff and got in. Whistles from the guys and "bye, Speedy," came through the open window. Robert ginned. "I see you've made friends already, Charlie."

Worry about Donnelly distracted me. "Just guys. Hey, I made the track team."

Chapter 9

Running up the stairs, one goal in mind, I tossed books and gear on the bed and unearthed my old backpack from the depths of the closet. A frantic search and I found it. Patrick Donnelly's card. Just as I pictured. Same last name as Thomas, football player at the fancy high school I just enrolled in. How to find out if they're related? I could ask Uncle if he knew about a detective in Thomas' family. No. Better to find a private way. There must be a computer in the house. They have everything else.

I sat chilled on this hot summer day with the possibility of discovery all because of a chance meeting. Thomas Donnelly didn't know my name yet but word gets around about a new girl. And why should I wig out? No reason for Patrick to connect me with. . .Nah. No way. Tell no one. Ever. Get close to no one. Ever.

My compulsion for neatness took over and I cleared a space of honor for new text books. Caressing each one, my stepping stones to success, they replaced classic Russian novels. Chekhov, move over. I emptied the gym bag of smelly gear and left my shoes to dry out.

A knock and Edgar's rich voice said, "Miss Charlie, two puppies need you."

I threw open the door, all worries forgotten for a minute with Lord and Lady racing in, excitement in every yip. Kneeling down to rub their bellies, I wound up on my back with the dogs licking my face and hands. In the middle of wagging tails and tumbling furry bodies, I caught a glimpse of shined black shoes nearby. I peered way up and there stood Edgar, an almost smile on his face.

"Thanks, Edgar. You're a sweetie for thinking of the pups." He turned to leave. "You know if there are computers in the house, don't you?"

"I do."

I waited. Nothing from the tight lipped man. "Are there?" I said

"Of course." He left. A man of few words.

I'd just learned two things. Be very specific when I asked Edgar a question and go to the source for information. After I walked the pups, I'd ask my aunt if she had the much needed computer.

Chapter 10

With her permission, an hour later I sat at Aunt Eleanor's neat desk and searched for information. Surprised to find Aunt Eleanor at ease as she booted up and showed me a few basics on her home computer, I wanted to call Mom and say, "She's years ahead of you. You wasted your life with. . ."

My aunt interrupted the dark thoughts. "Take as much time as you need, dear. Dinner is at seven."

Fists clenched, I wanted to punch myself for any bad ideas of Mom, a dumb sixteen year old when she ran away. Mental note: Ask Aunt if Mom went to Randolph High.

Thomas and Patrick Donnelly are brothers. After an hour of searching, the information jumped out. I should have gone to the police site. No biggie. Not much. Hands shaking so bad my fingers kept slipping off the keyboard. *Get me out of here.* I closed out the screen and sat. Think. I told Patrick, with a phony southern accent for god's sake, that my aunt worked here. Temples throbbed. Go on. Had him drop me off about four blocks north of here and I ran around to the back so he'd think I went to the servant's entrance.

For the first time since I went to communion at eight years old in a white second hand dress, I prayed. On my knees in this quiet room where my aunt trusted me, I prayed.

Forgive me please and keep my secret safe, God. I killed my father to protect my mother and she protected me by claiming self-defense and saying she hit him. Now I have a chance for a good life but I can't ever tell you in Church. I promise to be good, God. Just don't let Detective Patrick Donnelly suspect that I am anything but a decent person.

Head bowed, I remained on the plush flowered carpet for a long time until Edgar's voice called. "Six thirty, Miss Charlie."

Game face on, I opened the door.

RECONSTRUCTING CHARLIE

Tension at the dinner table made me nervous. Usually pleasant conversation flowed between Aunt and Uncle so I watched, waited, and ate another delicious meal, chicken sliced thin with mushrooms and lemon sauce, brown rice and broccoli. No grease. Wow.

Uncle cleared his throat. "Sorry I'm such a bear tonight. A new client, nasty bit of business." Digging in with forced energy, he said, " Charlie, did you make the track team? Betty Garrison is tough. She's been there a long time and owns the position."

"Yes." I left out the part where I almost ran into the next county obsessed with dear old Dad's image chasing me.

"Good."

"And are the team members pleasant? You're a newcomer and they're bound to be annoyed," Aunt Eleanor said, getting to the point.

"Annoyed isn't a strong enough word to express the, uh, hostility in the air when I out ran Lori, their number one."

"Hmm," she said. "Well, as I always say, they'll have to get over themselves. You're here to stay."

Uncle Stuart nodded in agreement. Robert served apple cobbler for dessert, compliments of Mrs. Appleton.

Mental note: Meet the chef and the rest of the staff.

"Did my mother go to Randolph High School?" I caught the exchanged glance between my favorite people.

Aunt Eleanor touched a long gold chain at her neck like the one mom gave me. "She did. As I told you, Elizabeth marched to a different beat and the tune was out of synchronization with school protocol. She did get up to mischief often." She turned the conversation over to Uncle Stuart.

"I bailed her out often. There were tears, she'd promise to conform and then, well, she met your father. He played guitar. She disappeared."

We sat quiet for a little while, digesting dinner and for me, the story of a wild mother.

Taking me by the arm, my dear uncle said, "Let's visit Lord and Lady. Time for fun.

Down the hall we went to the back yard. Uncle Stuart threw me another bone. "What do you think about a dog house? I know a carpenter. . ." Joyous barks greeted us. I almost howled with happiness.

Chapter 11

"Hey, what the hell? Track isn't a contact sport," I yelled after a push from the former number one spot, Lori.

I caught my balance and faced off with her, the team moving in to see what came next, Coach nowhere in sight. Stepping into her space, I said with a low growl, "Keep your fucking hands off me. Got it?" Her stony face cracked around the edges and she nodded.

Raising my voice a notch to include the team, I said, "I get it, okay. I'm new, you're the team. I came to run. That's all. You want to beat me, run faster. I don't give a shit."

The chug of a golf cart came closer. Coach called, "Are you planning a new strategy?"

Team captain Lori called back, "Uh, yeah, I guess."

On that happy note, the second day of practice ended.

Out of the gym roared the football team, hormones thick as fog. Thomas Donnelly, the only guy with half a brain according to Uncle Stuart, appeared to be in charge with all the black and gold helmets bent toward him.

In one quick move, Lori whipped off her visor and shook long blond hair back and forth. She watched way too many daytime dramas.

A few whistles cut the air. Thomas said something and had their attention.

"Damn. I'd do anything to have him plant his cleats under my bed."

"Anything?" Caroline, one of Lori's followers said.

Everyone giggled and I hurried to the locker room, in and out before anyone hit the shower.

"Bye, Charlie. See you tomorrow," a friendly voice called as I ran through the swinging doors to meet Robert.

RECONSTRUCTING CHARLIE

Someone said goodbye. How about that!

The someone turned out to be Lori, I figured out the next morning. She must have decided to befriend and disarm the enemy—me. No way would I ever be friends with her. Mom always said, "Hurt me once, shame on you. Hurt me twice, shame on me." In plain words, don't be a stupid fuck.

From the next day on, team spirit came first. Coach had nothing to yell about and her way of talking in capital letters all the time, changed to an occasional shout. As for me, I watched my butt.

My concern with the limousine suddenly ended when Uncle Stuart said he had an old car in good shape garaged not far from home. Home. I love the word. For my eighteenth birthday in May 1999, the car would be my gift. Two and a half years away.

"At your age, you may feel eighteen is too far away. Be patient. Life for you here holds new discoveries and the time will pass quickly."

We were in Uncle Stuart's study, a room I'd love to sleep in to inhale the knowledge from all of the leather bound books lining the shelves. Through osmosis. Breathe it all in except for heavy lemon polish used to shine each surface. Geez! I could do a better job with a dust cloth.

"Of course, there are contingencies," he said, voice clearing much improved since Lord and Lady moved in. "Nothing you can't accomplish, my dear. All A's in every subject and mind your p's and q's."

I laughed so hard, tears fell. "Uncle, p's and q's refer to pints and quarts left at pubs so drinkers had their own mugs."

His face reddened. "Of course. I knew that. It was a test and you passed. Your first A. Now go along and try to keep a stiff upper lip when Robert transports you at your beck and call. In a limousine."

After stashing my gym bag in the women's locker room, I hurried to class #1, first day of school. US History. I planned to sit in the back but a semicircle arrangement made that impossible. Eight a.m. sharp, the teacher, a woman, not old like teachers back home, decked out in the latest vest, white blouse and skirt outfit, strode in to greet fifteen students.

"Good morning, I'm Ms. Berg. We'll begin by studying pre-colonial origins."

I'd read the first section of the book, paid attention to her and took notes. Suddenly a bluebird flapped its wings against the floor to ceiling side window startling everyone. It made a lazy circle in the air and flew away. A good omen. The class used the bird as an excuse to talk but my eyes were drawn to the outside. I noticed the tips of leaves had turned color already changing the appearance of the old oak trees nearby.

A sharp rap on her desk and Ms. Berg re-captured the class. Forty minutes later, my head buzzing with information, a bell rang. The rustle of papers, a rush for the door, and the room emptied

"Miss Costigan, a moment, please."

Uh oh.

Ms. Berg said, "Welcome to our school. I saw your test grades. Very impressive. I look forward to stimulating contributions from you this semester." She smiled showing an overbite. Kind of cute. I hurried to the next class knowing my reputation preceded me. And so the morning went.

Lunch could be taken outside. I found a bench under a tree, unpacked a peanut butter sandwich, apple, apple juice, and a napkin. Gourmet style. No Ms. Appleton around when I crept into the sparkling kitchen and made it all by myself.

A guy threw his backpack next to mine interrupting my privacy.

Uninvited, he said, "Hey Speedy, Joey Moreland here." He offered a beefy hand for a handshake. I bit into my sandwich. "Okay, if I sit here?" He unwrapped the biggest hero sandwich I'd ever seen and tore off a chunk, lettuce hanging from this mouth. "The guys and I made a bet about you. The one who gets to talk to you first wins the pool. But you gotta answer back. See?"

He pointed to a group of guys a couple of trees away. They looked as if they should be swinging from branches, munching on leaves, nuts, bananas. The football team.

"So far you didn't talk so please, Speedy, say something."

Mentally I said, "Get the fuck away or I'll kick you in the balls," but he looked okay. Not a bad guy. I said, "My name's Charlie Costigan. I'm a private person so please leave me alone."

He appeared startled like no girl had ever turned him away before. Mumbling sorry, he packed up and left. I finished lunch and concentrated on the afternoon agenda. Two more classes, the first track meet on home turf at four. Get to the locker early to check on my gear. Stretching my calves, I rotated ankles nice and easy admiring my running shoes just about broken in. Feet and shoes were becoming best friends.

Adding to the tension; first day of new school, team competition moved to first day as well, I entered English Eleven early, sat in the back row and Thomas Donnelly slid into the seat next to me. He didn't glance over to say hello. Just opened the text book and buried his slightly upward tilted nose in it. No coming on to me like most guys. Hmm. Well, I wouldn't have to beat him off with a stick.

Mrs. Drummond talked about electives; a choice between Journalism and Creative Writing. We had two days to decide. Creative Writing hit me just right. Disguise the story and get it off my chest. Not possible. Make the safer choice--Journalism. The minute the bell rang forty minutes later, Thomas shot out of the room with me a close second, almost hitting me with the swinging door.

Classes over, I headed to the locker room with a sense of excitement. I stopped, chilled by the sight of my locker. The big room empty with no witness to the vandalism; broken door, lock open, gym bag unzipped, team uniform torn. Fury rose inside me ready to explode. One hour before the meet. One hour.

I called home. "Edgar, is my aunt there?"

"She has gone out. What may I do for you?"

Holding back tears, I said, "This is an emergency, Edgar. Please go to my room, top dresser drawer and take out a sports bra. At the back of the closet is a backpack. Grab an old pair of blue jeans and a tee shirt and hurry. Meet me at the main entrance to the high school. And Edgar, bring a sharp scissors. Thank you."

"Roger." The line went dead.

Did he say Roger?

Talk about influential, ten minutes later a police motorcycle, red lights flashing, led the way for the limousine—Robert at the wheel-- to pull up to the main entrance. Edgar made his elegant way, case in hand as I sprinted over and reached way up to kiss him on the cheek.

"Thanks, I owe you one."

In a toilet stall, I struggled into the bra top and covered up with an old tee shirt. Next came the hardest part, cutting the legs off my fave jeans from long ago. "Sorry, kids," I said and slashed right through the threadbare fabric. Funky but it would have to do. Hair up in a ponytail, I prepared to run my ass off. Something rattled around in the case. I found a cold bottle. Almost giddy, I guzzled the juice drink Edgar packed, one of Aunt Eleanor's specials. I caught my reflection in the mirror and said, "Charlie Costigan—no loser here."

At the track, eyebrows raised to the max, Betty Garrison said, "What the hell are you wearing?"

I felt the team grow quiet waiting for my answer.

"Sorry, Coach, there was an accident with my gym bag, the team uniform is ruined. Lucky someone from home brought something for me to wear."

She didn't buy it but just then a bus pulled up with the opposition. If we won, she'd bend a little. If we lost, well maybe she'd blame it on my clothes. When she hurried to greet the arriving team and their coach, I took the time to look in every one of my team member's eyes.

I said, "We're going to win today and put this crap behind us. Got it? But I want you all to remember one thing. I won't ever forget or forgive what you've done." Slowly one by one, they nodded. I added a little boost. "Go team all the way."

After beating the hell out of the other team, then shaking hands with them, I saw a familiar face in the cheering crowd. Patrick Donnelly. An icy fist clutched my heart. He waved and walked across the field. Beads of sweat changed to a river from every pore. Tearing off my tee shirt, I mopped up as if I always perspired like this. Dark clouds rolled in and a strong wind blew. Rain coming.

"Hi, Charlie Costigan. Good race," he said.

"Thanks, Patrick. How come you're here today?" As if I didn't know he'd come to see little brother.

"My brother Tom is on the football team. I come by once in a while." He grinned. "Are you eighteen yet?"

He's not bad. He doesn't suspect. . . .or.

"Not yet."

He leaned close. "Lost your southern accent, did you?"

I mopped my face again to hide the fear. "Just being dopey, I guess. New in town like fresh off the boat in a big city."

"When I got into the academy, I was a dope so I know what you're talking about. Looks like you'll do well here. Good luck, Charlie." Patting my wet shoulder, Patrick moved on.

My gut told me this wouldn't be our last meeting.

Coach called my name. I hurried over.

"You ran a good race today. I'll have a new uniform for you by next week." We walked together without speaking for a minute. "There's more to what you said about the gym bag accident, right?"

I kept on moving without a word. When she left me to go in the locker room, I phoned Robert.

Chapter 12

"Thanks to Edgar, I ran a good race today," I said as dinner came to a close.

This end of the day special time gave me a chance to get a feel of what love between a couple should be. I listened to conversation between Aunt and Uncle and knew I wanted it for myself. I wouldn't settle for anything less. If I even got close enough to anyone to find out.

They looked up from vanilla pudding with raspberries.

"What do you mean, dear," Aunt Eleanor said.

I had decided to tell the whole track story to them. Too many secrets for me to handle and word might get around.

Uncle Stuart frowned after I finished, brows forming a deep crease. "And you didn't report the vandalism to the coach?"

I shook my head. "I dealt with it my own way. They won't bother me again."

He smiled. "You might consider law as a profession, my dear."

After Lord and Lady snuggled in their bed next to mine at nine o'clock, already too tired to think or read, I turned out the light. Sleep came fast.

The nightmare returned. *A cold filthy hand reached for me and I ran calling for help through alleys of garbage and rats. Men in overalls, boys in jeans with fly fronts open lurched from dark doorways, hands tearing at my clothes and I ran faster. The stink of whiskey and cigar smoke from Dad's clothes making me choke. Air. I needed air.*

I woke up drenched in sweat with the puppy's rough tongues licking my tears until I stopped crying. The white telephone on the night stand, unused since I'd moved in, called to me. I punched in Mom's number.

She picked up, her voice breathless. "Mom, is he really dead? "I said and cried some more. We'd been so close until she made me run away.

"Oh, Charlie." Quiet on the line. "My darling girl. Yes. It's our secret to keep forever. Make sure you never tell anyone. I could get in a whole lot of trouble for lying."

Mom in trouble? Never thought she'd get in trouble. "I promise."

"Yes, Charlie. Oh, my girl. Are you all right?"

"Yes. It's great here, Mom. I miss you and the kids." I cried harder. "Mom, are you all right?"

"Yes, I'm fine. I have some good news. Remember the nice man I cleaned house for, Max Calhoun. His wife died a few years ago."

She's going to tell me Max Calhoun wants to marry her and move far away. To a good place. I knew it deep inside me.

And that's what Mom told me as I listened with tears falling and my Labradoodles licking them as fast as they fell.

"In two months," she said, "maybe November we're going to take the kids and move to Utah where Max has a spread."

Far away from Chicago and far away from our secret. Again she said I shouldn't call, she'd call me. Again she said she loved me. Again she said goodbye. Little pieces of my heart fell off and I didn't know how to put them back together.

After changing into a clean tee shirt and panties, I climbed between the silky sheets to find Lord and Lady still there, tails wagging. Against my better judgment, did I have any at fifteen? I let them curl against me, their warm furry bodies a comfort. My last waking thought: tell Aunt and Uncle about the long distance call and offer to pay the charge.

Heavy rain pounding the windows matched my wake-up mood. I showered off my grief and realized I had a new life, now Mom had one. No sense wasting energy over what I couldn't control. Move on. And I made a plan for a little independence. With two hundred forty two dollars in my money belt, I'd buy a bike to solve the immediate limousine embarrassment. Lots to talk about over dinner tonight.

No time to waste, mind in a spin, I dressed in the short skirt outfit, scooted two reluctant pups out to the covered run in the back and hurried to slap a pb and j sandwich together for lunch.

To my surprise, the kitchen buzzed with activity. Irish music played and made me want dance as a woman wrapped in a crisp white apron stirred with a long handled wooden spoon, what smelled like soup. Potato soup. And not just a regular woman. So pretty with black hair pinned up, some freckles, and blue eyes. A little shorter than me with a good shape. Almost as good as mine and she must be a lot older.

"Good mornin' to you, Charlie. It's time we met. I've lunch for you on the counter," she said, gesturing to a blue insulated lunch pack, something I always wanted, with the spoon dripping soup on the floor.

I quick wiped the drips with a paper towel.

"I'm Ms. Appleton. Call me Granny Apple. All me kiddies call me by the sweet name. A better lunch is packed than your humble peanut butter and jelly and ready to go. Now have some pancakes and be on your way."

Her Irish brogue swept away last night's sadness.

"Thanks so much, uh Granny Apple, for lunch and the lunch pack."

Delicious pancakes finished, I said, "Thanks. Oh, just one more question, please?"

An arched eyebrow raised, she nodded giving me permission to speak in her kitchen.

"Do you know who does laundry here? I'm not used to all the service and want to thank her for washing my clothes."

"'tis Sean, me nephew." Granny Apple's eyes flashed a warning and turned back to stir the soup.

Sean. A guy is washing my personal stuff. Touching my underwear. My blood boiled. What to do? I left for school.

Chapter 13

"Junior year is the most important time for students. Of course, Randolph High School has the highest SAT scores in the country and all of our students continue to higher education." The principal, Mr. Adams, went on and on looking very impressed with himself. Finally the informative speech ended, students dismissed to hurry to their next class. I had Biology. Preoccupied with the laundry situation, I almost reached the classroom on the second floor when a big guy blocked my path. In the crowded corridor, at first I thought it might be an accident but when my shoulders were pinned against the wall and he said, "I'm Brad Purvis. How about going to a movie this Friday night?" I knew he meant it.

Between clenched teeth, I said, "Get away from me."

A hand snaked around Brad's thick neck and shoved him aside as if he weighed ten pounds instead of over two hundred. Thomas Donnelly's voice said, "No way to treat a lady, Brad." And my hero entered the room I'd been heading for. I could have handled the guy myself but no one knew how tough Charlie Costigan could be, except for the track team.

Once again, we sat side by side with the football team's captain never glancing my way, both with noses buried in over-sized text books. I scribbled THANKS on a post-it, reached over and stuck it to Thomas' book. He bobbed his head once and read on. What the hell? I'd gotten more of a rise from a geezer than from this guy. His brother paid more attention to me than. . .I did not want to think about why Patrick Donnelly might pay attention to me.

Still raining and by the end of class I didn't have a clue about where to take my lunch. I'd been eating outside after practice but not today. I didn't know anyone else and Thomas sat next to me. So I wrote another note, WHERE DO I TAKE MY LUNCH? and stuck it to his book.

Obviously annoyed, he shook his head and longish blond hair fell across wide shoulders. He wrote CAFETERIA DOWNSTAIRS-FOLLOW YOUR NOSE and slapping the note on my book just as the bell rang, he made a dash for the door.

Follow my nose? As soon as I got downstairs I understood. Powerful over-cooked food smells filled the air. I found a quiet corner and opened my new lunch pack. Granny Apple had prepared a feast complete with cloth napkin, a real fork and knife. Smiling to myself, I spread out a small antipasto dish with cheese, olives, thin sliced ham, and tomatoes. All great stuff. Plus a bottle of Aunt Eleanor's special juice.

Lost in the pleasure of knowing people looked after me in a good way, I didn't notice company at the table. Suddenly flanked by two big guys I recognized from the football team, I wondered why they'd sit here.

"Hey," I said, "what brings you over to this corner of the cafeteria?"

"Marv," he said, "I'm Marv, he's Jesse." He gestured to the other guy. "Cap said to keep you company." He did a double take at my lunch. "Nice food," and unwrapped a King sized burger.

We sat in peaceful coexistence until I finished and said 'bye. *Cap said? He meant Thomas, captain of the team. Who never spoke or glanced at me. I thought I knew about men. . .and boys. Not all of them. . .maybe.*

Chapter 14

After school, like a sleuth I searched for Sean, launderer of my underwear, and found him in the basement doing his job. Marching down the stairs, detergent smells and other clean scents hit me. Step by step brought me into the cleanest basement I'd ever seen. I planned to tell him I'd take care of my personal stuff but when he heard my footsteps and turned, Sean grinned a lopsided-sided grin and stole my heart.

I'd seen kids like him back home, not too many but enough to recognize Down Syndrome. His blue eyes slanted a little upwards, face flattened just a bit and sweetness poured out.

"Miss Charlie," he said, his speech almost clear. Extending a hand, he said, "Hello."

I wanted to kiss and hug him, this boy earning money working for my aunt and uncle. Definitely educated, maybe as far as high school for all I knew. All my fears went up in smoke. We talked about the dogs, Sean loved them, clapping his hands as he talked about the way they licked his face. One of his jobs was to clean up the run each day. He said, "Phooey." Taking my hand, he showed me clean garden tools hanging on hooks.

"Clip flower heads outside," he said, pride showing on his face. "Lots of work to do," and he turned back to the washing machine.

I said, "Good bye," and never worried about my laundry again.

At six thirty, Aunt Eleanor knocked. "Come in." I said, "Is it time for dinner already? I'm not quite finished with tomorrow's English Eleven assignment."

She stayed at the doorway looking like a walking flower garden, beautiful in a pastel print Great Gatsby kind of dress with a handkerchief hemline.

"Let me guess. You and Uncle Stuart are going out and I'm going to eat in. . ."

"The kitchen with the staff. Won't that be fun? You've already met Ms. Appleton and Sean and Robert and I believe even Edgar will join you. In fact, it sounds like more fun than we'll be having at a stuffy fundraiser downtown. But go we must."

"I have something important to tell you," I said, Mom's news on my mind.

She paused. "We should be home by eleven. That's too late for you. Let's have a date for tomorrow after school or dinner. Call me." With a rush of silk, on light footsteps my aunt came close and brushed a kiss across my forehead, her floral scent left behind.

Reliving the moment, I closed my book. Later for you, I promised. I washed up and headed to the kitchen.

Aromas of potato soup and maybe pot roast, sent my salivary glands into overdrive.

"Just time," Sean said and clapped his hands when I hurried in.

"You're late," Robert said.

I sat next to Edgar, happy to be with the staff, my kind of people.

Granny Apple surveyed her domain. She said, "Something's missing, Sean."

He grinned his dear way and loped out the door returning a few minutes later with Lord and Lady. Dogs in the kitchen. A surprise at every turn in this house.

"When the cat's away, the mice will play," Edgar said and reached to scratch two curly headed pups.

I said, "Sit, stay," and pointed to the floor. They did. "I'm an experienced waitress so I volunteer to serve."

Sean clapped his hands.

"No. 'Tis so kind for you to offer but unseemly. You are a guest this night," the excellent chef said.

"Please let me help. All I do around here is take and I'd really like to give back once in a while."

Again Sean clapped then grabbed a spoon and clinked it against his glass.

"You're it tonight, then," Granny Apple said, removing the white apron.

Wow, what a neat figure. She probably doesn't sample too much of her own cooking.

She continued. "Begin with soup. On this rainy day into night, the house takes on a chill. Got to ward off colds with soup, don't you know. And a bit of pot roast never hurt."

I ladled and served, sat and ate, and became part of the whole household. No longer just the niece who showed up from nowhere.

At one point Granny Apple said, "Edgar, I see what you're doing."

Edgar's lips formed a tight line and his eyebrows went up.

"Don't you go looking all innocent on me now. You're sneaking food to the dogs under the table like a thief in the night, you are." She smiled. "I don't blame you but better to mash the carrots. They're just pups."

Oh, this is more fun than anything I'd done since coming here.

After dinner, while Robert cleared and cleaned up with Sean's help, I decided to ask for advice. About dating.

Without giving away past experience, I said, "A few football players have asked me to go out. On dates." All heads turned my way. "I have a plan and I'm asking you all to listen and tell me what you think."

Sean and Robert dried their hands and sat at the table.

"Okay. I'm not really into dating because back home, well, I had some unpleasant experiences. But I'm starting new here and if a girl doesn't go out after guys keep asking, uh, there might be gossip. And kids can be mean."

Everyone nodded.

"So here's my plan. I accept a date to the movies because then I don't have to talk too much to the guy and a movie is a safe place. And after the movie, he takes me for a snack someplace and then it's time to go home. And maybe he thinks because he spent money on me, now he can, uh expect something in return but when he drives me home, Edgar opens the door and does his Edgar thing and the guy knows he better leave. So I say thanks and good night. And I'm home. Safe." I took a deep breath and waited.

"What exactly is my Edgar thing," Edgar said.

"Oh, you know. You wear a black suit looking serious like you're in charge of the house," I said.

"All true. I believe your plan will work, Miss Charlie."

"I'll get pepper spray for you," Robert said.

Granny Apple said, "I do believe that's illegal."

"Maybe so. I'll get two cans."

"Dessert time," Sean said.

Apple pie. Delicious.

Homework finished and ready for bed at ten thirty, I heard Aunt Eleanor call to me at the door.

"Come in." Lord and Lady stirred in their bed but didn't wake up.

"Is this a good time, dear? We were bored and Stuart wanted to come home. You said you had something to tell me."

Well this might be the perfect time to get the conversation with Mom off my mind.

Peering at my aunt in the dim light of the room with rain splashing against the big windows, I knew Mom's decision to send me here could only bring good luck.

"I had a nightmare last night," I said fighting back tears, "and when I woke up, I called Mom. I know she said not to call but, uh, I had to hear her voice to know she was okay."

"Is she?"

"Well, she said she is. She's more than okay is what she said. A nice man she used to clean house for, a widower, is going to marry her in a few months and they're. . ." Tears I couldn't stop, poured like a leaky faucet. I grabbed tissue and mopped up before the pups had a chance to jump on the bed. "They're moving to Utah. He has something Mom called a spread. Must mean a lot of land and she said not to call. She'd call. So they'll be gone. Far away. With my brother Jimmy and my two little sisters, Celia and Cary. And what if he's not the nice man she thinks he is?"

Aunt Eleanor muttered something under her breath. *Did she say bitch? Not possible. Not from Aunt Eleanor's mouth.* Then she reached for me, tears and all and pulled me close to her silk flower garden dress and didn't let go until the last tear gave up. Soon a cool wash cloth pressed against my cheek. It felt so special. And my aunt spread a thin layer of lotion all over my face with her gentle touch.

"Don't worry so much about your mother. She learned from her first mistake. Someday, before you know it, maybe we can bring your brother and sisters here for a visit. Stuart and I would love to meet them." She tucked the blanket under my chin and kissed my cheek. "Get a good night sleep, dear. See you tomorrow."

The door closed. Too late, I remembered the phone charge. I forgot to offer to pay the phone charge.

A few months later, Aunt and Uncle said they were pleased when my social life improved. And by the end of the first year with them, I had outgrown the guest room and they moved me into a kind of suite down the hall. Now I had a little study with a desk, computer and storage for school stuff and a larger bedroom because Lord and Lady had grown huge. Like four times their original size and they took up a lot of space.

If only Mom called or maybe she didn't care. I got rid of dear old Dad, she has this Max person and his spread in fucking Utah and my brother and sisters. Don't go there, Charlie. Don't let her mess up your head.

Chapter 15

March 1998

After a difficult cross country race where we jumped over rocks, broken fences, and at one point, a narrow stream, both teams gathered to shake hands. Coach called me aside.

"The new cross country coach from Northwestern wants to meet you."

My heart did a wild dance. Just what I'd hoped for.

As my team watched from a distance, they always kept their distance from me, I blotted sweat from my face and hands and hoped for the best.

The powerful woman had the authority of bringing a sport new to NU and she strode toward me, a grin on her face. No wasted motion, her body fine-tuned like the runner she was known to be. Coach always talked about prominent runners and Lynne Riley rated at the top.

"Well, hello Charlie Costigan. I'm Lynne Riley. I've heard a lot about you and now I've watched you in action. You're something. Where did you learn to dodge obstacles and regroup so quickly? You must have had a terrific coach early in your training."

What training? You'd run like me if you had dear old Dad for a coach. I jumped over garbage cans, dodged hands grabbing for me, drunks. . .

I just grinned right back like 'aw shucks and thanks.'

"We'd like you to join our cross country team. Practice begins in August but make sure you keep fit all summer." She looked me right in the eyes, "And I mean in the best shape."

In one hand she held a list of exercises for me to follow. I read. A specific strength and conditioning program, focus on hill and speed plus threshold running. *So much for leisure time this summer.* As if she heard my thoughts, Coach Riley said, "Summer is all about preparing your body for the more intense workouts in September. Coach Garrison said she'd work with you." A quick shake of my hand, "Welcome to our team, Charlie." I watched her disappear in a cloud of dust over the hill.

April and May

All through the spring, Uncle Stuart, Aunt Eleanor and I discussed Northwestern

University's curriculum until we were dizzy with too many choices. Uncle wanted me to get a taste for law; Aunt thought Liberal Arts to be a well-rounded beginning; and I, well I wanted to push buttons to the future where I envisioned myself as the head of. . .something. Something I designed and constructed. Indestructible and splendid. When I revealed my plans built of dreams, my favorite people nodded. They didn't laugh at a seventeen year old girl with big ideas and no substance. They believed in my ability.

"Speak to a guidance counselor," Uncle Stuart said. "They know what courses are required for freshmen and how to guide you toward your ultimate goal." He smiled a wicked Uncle Stuart smile. "Whoever gets the job of guiding our Charlie is in for a big surprise."

"Now, now, dear," Aunt Eleanor said. "Don't belabor the issue." She turned to me.

"Charlie, you will succeed in whatever direction you decide upon. Look how far you've come since you knocked on our door." Then she passed a dish of truffles around.

June

Almost two year ago, I showed up at this house on Lake Shore Drive with no idea of how I'd be received. Today, as I stepped into a long olive green dress the saleslady said looked perfect with my hair and Aunt Eleanor agreed, I left that fifteen year old girl behind. Graduation Day. Wow. A full scholarship to Northwestern based on my cross country record and academics. I twirled around feeling the slinky dress spread out from my hips down. Almost time to go.

I had tickets for everyone but Lord and Lady. My family. One of the ten most perfect days of the year, the weatherman said this morning with low humidity, temperature about seventy. Perfect for the outdoor ceremony. Carrying my cap and gown, I almost plummeted down the stairs in new clunky heel pumps.

Robert beeped the horn, Edgar stood by the limousine door to escort me inside where Aunt and Uncle sat beaming. Granny Apple and Sean smiled up at me. Edgar arranged his long legs in front and off we went. Room for everyone. For just a second, I wondered if Mom realized she hadn't called me since the night she said they were moving far away. Her loss. I willed the dark thought away.

The valedictorian, Thomas Donnelly, gave a speech about giving back to the community and volunteering whenever we could. Cheers erupted from the crowd. Admired by all, Tom, the guy who never spoke to me but had watched out for the new girl in his own quiet way. I'd miss him a lot.

When the names of the class were called, we had practiced this drill the day before, one by one we were to walk quickly across the stage to shake hands with the principal and receive the diploma. At that time any awards would be announced.

The loudspeaker called, "Charlie Costigan," and I had taken my place up and almost running across the stage, heard the announcement. "Highest SAT scores in our school history." I slowed down, reveling in the moment. Words I said when I got off the bus after that terrible night came back. "Chicago, do you hear me?" Applause broke out from the audience. I shook hands and thanked Mr. Adams, then waved my diploma in the air.

When Thomas received his diploma, the loudspeaker announced he had a full scholarship to Northwestern. Across the sea of friends and family, his blue eyes met mine. He grinned. For the first time in my life, I felt a small tingle low in my belly.

When the last student clutched his diploma, the band played as sixty five caps sailed up in the air to be caught by the wind. I had pinned a red ribbon on the underside of my cap and watched it take off while all around friends hugged, kissed and cried. My cap rose high like a rocket with a destination. Like me. Unaware the crowd broke up, drifting back to family, my focus stayed in the sky. A shadow blocked my sightline. I blinked and there stood Patrick Donnelly.

"Are you eighteen yet?" he said.

Annoyed that he broke my concentration, always nervous in his presence, I said, "No," remembered to smile and hurried to where my family waited.

RECONSTRUCTING CHARLIE

Aunt Eleanor, lovely as ever in peach chiffon, said, "Isn't that nice, dear. Thomas Donnelly will be going to school with you."

"I don't know him. We were in a couple of classes and sat next to each other and he never looked at me. I'm going there to work hard and study to be somebody. To make you and Uncle Stuart proud of me."

Uncle Stuart patted my back. "We're already proud of you, Charlie and just think, by earning a scholarship, you already saved us a bundle."

Edgar took pictures of the family, Robert and Sean played ball on the lawn and Granny Apple looked pleased to be out with all of us. She called me aside and pressed a small box in my hand.

"A little something to remember me by, dear girl."

Inside the box on a bed of satin, lay a gold pin in the shape of an apple.

Speechless, I could only hug the wonderful woman who cooked special meals to keep me strong and ward off evil spirits. I pinned it on my dress.

"This I've learned and give to you. Believe in the sun, even when it's not shining." A feathery kiss on my cheek and Granny Apple, graceful as always, left my side.

Chapter 16

Northwestern University

I'd visited the campus a few times and this day, my bags were open on the bed next to the window in the sunny room for two. Not used to sharing a space anymore, I dreaded what came next. A roommate. The thought of her gave me the shivers. And the idea of a co-ed dorm also made me uneasy. Lucky each room had an attached bathroom. Uncle Stuart assured me he'd pay extra for a single but I should give it a try. They spoiled me, those sweeties. I finished unpacking just as a key turned in the locked door. A life size Barbie the color of dark chocolate sailed in. A guy carrying too many bags trailed close behind.

Space invaders. This will never work.

Tossing what looked like a very expensive bag on the other bed, she ordered the guy to leave the bags and get lost. He did. Prepared to hate her, she blindsided me with a grin.

"Name's Shelley. Shelley Jackson. Basketball," and stuck out a hand with long tapered fingers I pictured wrapped around a ball. We shook hands.

"Charlie Costigan. Cross country."

"Oh, the new kids on campus. I heard about NU recruiting for women's cross country. Y'all must be fast. Y'all already proved it. Got here before me, grabbed the bed by the window."

I must have looked puzzled because she said, "Chill out. I won't be sleeping here too often."

My lucky day. "Who's the boyfriend?"

"The one who carried in my bags? That's Len. He's just one of them." And she unpacked twice as much as I brought on this first trip to college.

The August day called me outside to explore. Key, bills and coins in my fanny pack, I headed out into sunshine and a stiff wind. Classes didn't start until next week but cross country practice began tomorrow and this day might be my one free time to check out the town. Walk east to watch waves splash over the rocks along Lake Michigan or west to town? I tossed a coin and said heads for the lake. Heads won.

I fell in love half a block away from the dorm when I ran up the path and caught the lake in all its' splendor. Majestic in size, the dark blue water rolled with huge waves beaten by the wind. My breath caught at the beauty and power. Living on Lake Shore Drive, I'd been to the lake many times but never had a moment when no crowds were around. A sight to write back home about. *No. No more back home. I live here in Chicago with my aunt and uncle.*

I ran 'til I got over a flash of sadness. Tree lined streets provided welcome shade. Examining a leaf, the word poplar came to mind; tall and full, turned yellow gold in the fall. Turning a corner I found colorful booths set up with music coming from somewhere; all kinds of crafts were there with vendors dressed in ethnic costumes. Kind of a hippie feel to the street.

I fingered some hammered earrings, big dangles not my style and thought better of it. Drawn to a small painting of a horse with blinders on at another booth, I knew I had to buy it. After a long haggle, the artist agreed to let it go for twenty bills. Brown paper wrapping tied with a string. Mine. I'd hang it over my desk as a reminder to focus straight ahead. Happy, I swayed to the guitarist strumming, "Where have all the flowers gone" as I browsed, caught up in the atmosphere until a guy grabbed my hand and began to dance. I yanked free, caught the smell of pot wafting nearby and switched gears. Lots of restaurants on the street, some upscale and one spilled out with students. The Pub. Must be the place to go. I'd be too busy to spend much time hanging out anywhere and made my way back to the dorm.

Without a campus map, new and confused, I found myself at the north end standing in front of the entrance to a garden. My nose led the way, inhaling floral scents as if I'd stumbled into a perfume factory. A huge ancient stone plaque said Shakespeare Garden, dedicated 1916. There were a lot more words, too many to comprehend at the moment because I entered a different land of serenity and knew I'd found my place at Northwestern. At first, I wandered through to admire yellow daisies and golden marigolds too many to count. Rosemary, thyme and spikes of lavender grew lush against dark green leaves. I'd have to read about the garden to know all the plants by name and make friends.

Someone, an interloper to my privacy, sat on a stone bench not far from me, nose buried in a text book. Dressed in football gear, helmet in the grass at his feet, sat Thomas Donnelly. He didn't look up and I don't know why but picking up a pebble from the path, I tossed it at his helmet. The sudden ping made him lift his head. Hell, it startled me. I waggled my fingers hello. We stared at each other for a long minute and he grinned.

"Hi," he said. "You okay?"

I nodded and moved on to explore the garden. A line from an old movie Aunt and Uncle introduced me to flitted through my mind. "Of all the gin joints, in all the towns, in all the world, he walks into mine." I shook my head. I figured we were destined to cross paths as strangers. *Deep thinker, Charlie.*

After a peaceful exploration of the garden, I headed back to find the dorm and maybe learn more about my wild roommate Shelley, passing the still engrossed Thomas on the way. *No more pings for you, Tom.*

Chapter 17

Gone, the self-assured arrogant beauty, and in her place a teary eyed girl looking forlorn and maybe homesick.

"Hey Shelley, you're just what I need. I don't know about you, but this is a big school and I got lost a few times and I'm hungry. How 'bout you?" I opened some drawers for a change of clothes and pulled out shorts, a tee shirt and clean underwear.

Shelley sniffled. "What I said before, all bull shit."

"Oh. I believed every word." I sat at the edge of my bed removing my sneakers. "So you're not a sleazy slut sleeping around and I'm stuck with you?"

"Yeah."

"Get dressed and let's check out the Dining Hall."

Clothes in hand, I beat Shelley to the bathroom, showered and changed and came out in ten minutes. Blew dry my hair, added a bit of make-up and picked up a book to study. Introduction to Law.

Half an hour later, Shelley pranced out starkers, the word my little brother Jimmy used whenever our twin sisters ran around naked. She tossed a wet towel on the floor and searched for clothes to wear. I dressed in the bathroom and my roommate thought nothing of nakedness in front of me, a stranger. One of us had a lot to learn.

"Uh, Shelley, let's establish a ground rule here. I hope you plan to pick up the towel and keep the bathroom neat."

The smallest bikini panties I'd seen outside of a catalog were now on her body and she wiggled into a short shiny white skirt. A white stretch boob tube thing, the latest fashion, topped off the outfit and she tied the laces of white sneakers.

"Neatness counts, y'all," she said with a grin and like magic, the offensive towel hung on a rack to dry.

Concentration gone, I closed the book and waited, stretched and waited some more.

"What?" she said, poking earrings the size of basketball hoops through her ears.

"You look so. . ." Words failed me.

"So hot?"

I dug into my bottom drawer, found the lacy black and white scarf Corinne, the helpful sales woman had shown me how to tie. On tiptoes, I draped it around Shelley's neck, made the adjustments and stood back to see the result.

"Bare." I said. "Now you look like the campus hottie. Let's go."

Her big black eyes watered up. "That's something Grandma would've done. Thanks."

I learned a lesson the first day on campus. Friendships come in different sizes and shapes, and sometimes even color. Mine came six feet one inch tall, beautiful inside and out, and before long I found out, loyal. Charlie Costigan never had a friend before. Times were changing.

Unaware of her power, Shelley stopped traffic in the Dining Hall. Cutlery bounced off the parquet floor, a dish shattered and all because she entered the huge room. Her concentration focused on the food and she filled both our trays with fresh fruits, steamed vegetables, whole grain bread and pasta. I pictured Granny Apple's meals and now Shelley took over in the care and feeding of me. I don't know how the dorm people figured out roommate pairing, but I thanked them.

A table in the center appeared to be empty. We hustled over and claimed it. Before long, other trays clattered down. Young men slid into oak chairs and getting-to-know-you began.

One eager guy leaned across the table to get Shelley's attention. "Where do you come from? Uh, both of you."

I ignored him since he didn't care if I came from Mars. Between healthy bites, at home with small talk, Shelley said, "Alabama. English and Psych major concentrating on losing my southern accent."

I'm sure they were more interested in what else she'd lost, like virginity, but she kept the conversation light and fun. With my background, I'd never be comfortable with guys. Maybe I could learn to fake it by listening to Shelley.

An offer to escort us to The Pub for a brew made me cringe. A pinch from my roommate and we went with an entourage of six guys. We turned down the beer, ordered iced tea in the crowded restaurant bar and watched the college scene whirl around us. What a kick. A bunch of wanna-be-hotties trying to make out, make friends, make good before classes began. A lot of them jocks obvious from body tone, or summer school students.

"Fun, huh?" Shelley said.

"I think so." Yeah, a bit of fun. "Can't stay too long. Practice begins tomorrow."

She flashed a grin, bounced an invisible ball. "Me too."

Goodbyes waved to the nice guys who weren't ready to leave and back to the dorm we went.

"Y'all don't like crowds." Shelley said.

"No."

"Y'all don't like strangers bumping up against you."

"Don't go there, okay?" Uncomfortable silence followed for a block. "I've been a closed book for years."

"When you're ready to open the book, I'm here."

Chapter 18

Gone before sleeping beauty opened her eyes, I waited in the gym with Coach Riley and watched a group of young women straggle in at 7 a.m.

"Step lively," Coach called and blew the whistle hanging around her neck for the first time, a sound we learned to respond to like Pavlov's dog. The sound reverberated around the cavernous gym. How a small silver whistle commanded attention remained a mystery to me. A woman of average stature, maybe ten years older than me, and Coach Lynne Riley held us in the palm of her hand. My role model. From then on, whenever I'd hear a whistle blow, my feet itched to run.

We, referring to the team, had a nice ring to it. Me the loner no more. And we all resembled each other, in lean shape, pony tail hair-do, intense and later, when we suited up in the purple uniforms, we were something to watch.

As a freshman, I didn't expect to win in competition. Everyone else had experience in major events, travel to other colleges, coverage by television. Scary stuff. I just ran fast. At first, my confidence level dropped and Coach took me aside.

"Charlie, I saw you run and knew you were right for our team. What's the problem? A guy thing or do you have your period?"

I toed the ground, raised dust and looked ashamed.

"Talk to me."

"I don't have experience like the other girls. All those people yelling, the crowds."

She handed over a bottle of water and said, "Sit down. I think I know what the problem is." We drank. "You have stage fright." Nodding to herself, she continued. "An actor learns her lines yet when the curtain goes up, she forgets or is too nervous to get them straight. So here's what we're going to do."

RECONSTRUCTING CHARLIE

My sorry head drooped.

"Look at me when I'm talking to you. I want to see the fire you ran with when we met. We're going to have a cross country meet at Purdue soon and I expect great results from you. But first we'll have a rehearsal," she grinned, "with a big audience, get other teams to come, get the band out, make it a big deal competition right here and you, Charlie Costigan, are going to run your ass off. And love it. Because that's what it's all about, kid. Running is fun and a way of life for a real runner."

My tears fell. I never knew people ran for fun. I ran for my life. The association I made with running fast had to do with escaping dear old Dad. My secret.

Coach lifted my chin. "Why are you crying? Speak to me."

Deep breath for the big lie. Not too far from the truth but far enough for Coach to get a picture. Change the characters.

"Back home, there was, uh, a bully, who chased me. The only way I could get home safe was to run faster than him. And that's how I started. No fun. I just ran to survive."

Thoughtful, Coach stood and yanked me up. We headed out of the gym, my heart beating extra fast. At the double doors, she gave me a hard look. "Don't live in the past, Charlie. You have the power to make or break your future. And we are going to have an event the likes of which NU has never seen before."

In the Shakespeare Garden, I sat on the stone bench, thought about our conversation and recalled an interview I'd seen on television. A golf professional talked about how he approached each tournament. "I pictured the ball as a bird and when I connected with my driver, it flew down the fairway. Then when it came to putting, I visualized the hole on the green to be the size of a manhole cover and putted one right in."

The key to winning might be visualization. Sure, I trained hard but mental attitude is the most important ingredient after the training and practice. With the help of Coach and desire to win, I made a plan. Yeah, I made a lot of plans and most of them worked out.

True to her word, one week later the campus buzzed with news about a track relay and hurdles competition. The band playing and door prizes galore. Posters went up for the free event.

I hadn't known her very long but this turned out to be Coach Riley at her best. And she did this for me.

The sun blessed us after a week of cloudy with showers and the stadium filled to the band playing, "You're Still The One." All the athletes were there, boisterous, having a ball as if they were about to watch a major event. Shelley waved from the sidelines when we took the field to be introduced. Party time.

We competed against each other that day.

Shutting out the carnival atmosphere, where vendors sold hot dogs, soda and popcorn; a tall clown carried colorful balloons, peanut and popcorn hawkers yelled, I went into deep concentration and became a powerful bird. "Focus."

The beat of wings against my body, skimming the path, now airborne over the hurdle to stretch way out then skim feather-like faster to the higher obstacle and repeat the pattern faster, lean into the breeze to claim the next.

I almost ran into the bleachers when a whistle blew. The race ended. With joy in my heart, I ran my fastest time and won in hurdles, placed second in relays. A big presentation afterward, an interviewer with a microphone asked me how I felt winning my first time out, "Great," I said, applause from the crowd.

I hugged Coach. "Thanks for this."

"You found your fire, Charlie. Good work. Next time, after you cross the finish line, slow down."

Finish line? I didn't remember a finish line.

My teammates were high-fiving all over the place, toasting each other with bottled water, and they wanted to celebrate someplace local and cheap. I backed out and scanned the thinning crowd. An amazing day. When I searched for my roommate, a standout in a long sleeve green tee shirt, plaid short skirt and high black boots, she and Patrick Donnelly were in what appeared to be intimate conversation. A chance meeting or planned by the detective? A shadow fell across my happiness. I shook it off and made my way across the field to them, a smile and a wave to people streaming by.

Me, happy-go-lucky Charlie.

"We meet again," Patrick said. "Great job out there, Charlie."

"Hey. I knew y'all could do it." Shelley gave a big hug. "What a fine afternoon."

RECONSTRUCTING CHARLIE

A chill ran through me and I pulled on my track suit for warmth. Leaves began to fall as the wind picked up. One landed in Shelley's hair. Pat removed it, touching her cheek. Waves crashed against boulders at the lake so loud I heard them half a block away. Tonight was fall back night where you lost one hour. Already the sunny afternoon faded or maybe my over-stimulated imagination thought so. I needed a shower and a hot meal. And now my brand new friend and roommate stood before me with a guy I might have reason to fear. I figured we'd celebrate my success tonight.

"I'll head back now. Nice seeing you again, Pat."

His hand touched mine. "I'm working tonight. Funny how Shelley and I met." They shared a smile. "I came over to see Tom. You remember Tom, don't you, Charlie? And Shelley needed rescuing from some football players so I did what any good cop would do."

Suckered in for his punch line, I said, "What did you do, Pat?"

"Flashed my badge, they backed off and we met."

What a crock and Shelley liked it.

"I'll call you," he said, not to me. Gone in the crowd.

My turn to look at Shelley. "You needed rescuing?" We both laughed.

"He liked to think that. Yeah." We laughed all the way to the dorm and up to our room.

Running shoes off, track suit hung up, I gathered clothes to take in the bathroom.

Shelley had a way of being motionless and she sat, still and calm. On my way to the shower, her words stopped me. "Y'all are concerned about Pat. Frightened he might learn something about you."

I don't know how she sensed this but she did and I had to lie, kind of. Back to the edge of my bed, I said, "When I got off the bus in Chicago two years ago, I used a southern accent to get a ride. I figured he'd be nicer to a southern girl new in the city."

She said nothing.

"And when we got a few blocks from where I was going, I told him to let me off. My aunt worked there and told me to come around to the back entrance."

She said nothing.

"That's it." *Not really but enough.*

"Why did you lie?"

"Because I didn't want a stranger to know my aunt and uncle's address."

"Okay. I get it." In one languid move, she stretched out and closed her eyes. "He's a real man."

Showering fast, I got ready for dinner. Lying made me hungry.

Lots of laughter on the bus ride to Purdue but not from me as waves of hidden memories returned to haunt me. *Mom packs a suitcase with an old dress of hers inside, hands me a letter to relatives I never knew existed and says run, catch the last bus to Chicago, and all the time, Dad's back there in the kitchen, blood everywhere, his eyes empty staring at nothing. . .*I bit into a ham sandwich, looked out the window pretending to be a regular seventeen year old girl and prayed. *Please give me the courage to go on today, win with my team, and God, forgive what I did. I had to protect my mother. Amen.*

By the fierce expression on her face, I saw Coach knew something twisted inside me. When the sign said Welcome to West Lafayette and the Wabash River came into view, she stood up and gave us a pep talk.

"Listen up, folks. We've built a strong team even though we're the new kids on the block. A few of you haven't traveled as a team before. No big deal. Focus and you'll be great. Picture running the best you can and you will. Don't let anything stand in your way. What have we come here for?"

We shouted as a team, "TO WIN!

When our team ran out on the field, for some unknown reason I stopped, searched the stands and spotted Aunt Eleanor wearing a purple NU sweatshirt topped with a wide brimmed hat. Next to her sat Uncle Stuart in NU purple, for once no tie and jacket. My whole family sat in a row all dressed in purple; Edgar, Granny Apple and Robert sitting very close to her, and Sean who waved a purple flag and jumped up and down. They traveled all the way to support me.

That day I ran personal best for them as much as for me.

Chapter 19

After the successful track season ended, I decided to take the train home for the weekend. My first trip home and I missed everyone. Although we called each other, I hadn't seen them in a month. When Aunt and Uncle heard about my exceptional roommate, they invited her to spend Thanksgiving weekend.

College life had chewed me up and like Humpty Dumpty, I needed putting together again. On the way to the station, I passed a construction site and stopped. Like a movie moment where lights flash on and off and music swells to a crescendo, I had an epiphany. This is it. Tada! My dream of business and creating became clear.

Fascinated by the huge machinery, men in hard hats at work, I stepped on the path and walked closer. Someone yelled for me to get out. The sign said Duffy & Sons Construction, Inc. I strode up to the trailer where men were coming and going. The business office. Behind a battered desk, sat a powerfully built man with crew cut gray hair and wire rimmed glasses slipping down his nose every minute. A quick glance around the trailer told me everything I needed to know. A mess. Papers everywhere. He needed organization and I wanted to work here. To learn the business. This might be exactly what I'd dreamed of. I had a two hour window of opportunity a few days a week.

"Mr. Duffy?"

Head cocked, bushy eyebrows raised, he peered over his glasses. "That's me. I'm busy so make it fast. You lost your cat?"

I took a deep breath and said, "Mr. Duffy, you need my help."

His chair rolled back on squeaky wheels and he laughed so hard his face turned red.

"Do you have a business system to keep track of the employees, salaries, hours, expenses, construction costs, supplies?

"Young lady, I've been doing business forty years with this." He pointed to his head, a ledger, sharp pencils. "Who are you to walk in. . ."

"Sir, I didn't mean to insult you but this is 1998 and there's an easier and more efficient way to do business. Just give me two weeks to prove it. No salary and then we can talk. What do you say?"

He scratched his head, rolled the squeaky chair close, and said, "No salary for two weeks? What's the catch? Your daddy will come in and call the cops?"

Uh, no. Dear old Dad is where I put him.

"I want to learn the business, Mr. Duffy. This will be a good way to start. And who knows, someday you and I might be partners."

Removing his glasses, he wiped tears of laughter from his green eyes. We shook hands.

The trailer door banged open and a burly tall man marched in, stopped at the sight of me in a short skirt, boots and leather jacket.

"Hey Duff, who's the chick?"

My insides shivered at the word chick. Sexist pig.

"What's your name, Miss?"

"Charlie Costigan."

Mr. Duffy puffed out his chest like a rooster. "Meet Charlie, me new secretary."

"Office manager." I said. "See you Monday."

Lord and Lady turned themselves inside out when I walked in. Oh the wagging, kisses, and loves from my furry pups warmed my heart. I dumped my backpack on the entrance hall floor, sat down and let them put me back together again. By the time Aunt and Uncle came in, I had showered, changed and sparkled with news.

Over tea and apple turnovers, I told them about Duffy Construction and my plan. They always listened. No matter what craziness a teenager like me came up with, they still listened.

"And I offered to prove that in two weeks, with no salary, working a few hours after classes, Mr. Duffy's company would operate more efficiently." I scraped the last bit of apple cobbler from the plate and drained my cup. "Delicious."

Uncle Stuart cleared his throat before speaking. I thought the dogs helped his allergies or maybe I brought them back.

"Ken Duffy said all right to your plan? Ken Duffy Construction in Evanston on a big site now?"

"Dear, your face is red. We've got to watch your blood pressure," Aunt Eleanor said.

"Yes, he did. You know him?"

"We go way back, Charlie. He's tough. Made a bundle in construction. He's an ethical man."

"The sign says Duffy and Sons."

"Wishful thinking. They wanted children." He gave a sad shake of his head and gazed at Aunt Eleanor. "We have you but Ken and Shirley never had such good fortune."

"So what do you think?" I said, glancing from one to another, eager to get a reaction.

Robert filled Uncle's tea cup, the hint of a grin on his face. "As long as you maintain your grades. What's your feeling, my dear?" he asked Aunt Eleanor.

"I agree. Do watch out for the men. A tough bunch work in construction and they will resent a girl on the premises."

Her words struck home. "I will." Robert winked. His way to remind me of the pepper spray he'd given me last year. Mental note: *ask him for another one.*

When dinner ended, I said, "Is there an extra computer lying around somewhere? I'll need it to take to Mr. Duffy's next week. Would you believe he uses a ledger and a pencil, everything by hand? I want to set up an easy starter program."

I could see wheels turning, the light bulb go on and Uncle said, "I will loan one to you. Just a question here. When did you learn so much about computers, young lady?"

"I've followed the development and they had them at Randolph. Soon babies will learn how to use them."

He sighed. "I was born in the wrong century."

"How are you going to accomplish all that?" Dripping wet from a shower, hands on hips, Shelley scowled at me. "Too much ambition, not enough time."

"I can and will do it. Why? Because I need to, for me. Don't drip on my computer but look at my schedule. Here," I threw another towel at her, "A plan with all the hours accounted for."

"Hmm. I don't see time allotted for eating or sleeping."

"Shelley, lay off." Our first disagreement. She meant well. I'd met students who had plates overfilled by necessity and they

91

managed. Growing up prepared me for multi-tasking. "How's Pat?" Change the subject.

Again with the funny smile. "Oh, fine," and she slicked on body lotion, a dreamy expression on her face.

"How fine?"

"Are you fishing to find out if we've done it yet?"

Ice broken, we giggled and my dear roommate confessed a few intimacies. For a moment, I had a sense of losing her too soon and envy.

Dressed in pajamas, she sat next to me. "I'm not going anywhere, Charlie. Pat and I, well, it's a romance. We're not rushing into anything serious for a long time. Right now, I'm married to school. Basketball pays the tuition just like cross country pays yours. Academics come first and my goal requires years of study."

"Yeah, right. And if I believe that, do you have a bridge you want to sell?"

I became a master of the twenty minute nap break and by the end of two weeks, school and my job broke even.

Arriving at three p.m. the first day, catcalls followed me all the way to the office. I ignored, "Hey baby, fix this" and "Get a load of those knockers" though how anyone could see through my coat must have x-ray vision eyes. But when someone yelled, "I'd like a piece of your ass," I turned, stuck out my third finger, entered the trailer and slammed the door. The boss didn't look up. Used to brawny men stomping in and out all day, another slam made no impact.

Surveying the space situation, I found my niche in a lit corner. There I cleared the little desk of stuff to be sorted and filed, pulled up an extra chair, wiped everything clean with supplies in a cabinet under a stained sink and set to work. Mystified, Mr. Duffy peered at me over those dusty half glasses as if I came from outer space with a newfangled gizmo. His name for my donated-by-Uncle computer. From what Uncle Stuart told me, Duffy Construction could buy a bunch of computers—retail. I knew I'd have to ease him into the transition.

After an hour of programming the right one for his business, I stretched, had milk and a granola bar and asked the boss if I could check out his ledger. Like a virgin protecting his virginity, he paled.

"I promise I won't bite. I need to see how you run this big a business without help and show you I'm the one with the latest technology to save you money."

I saw from the spark in his eyes he liked the words—save money; the hook I used over and over.

I never planned to study accounting. Determination won out and I did over the weekend at home. Uncle Stuart asked his accountant to come over and give me a crash course. I learned enough to make an impression. What I observed after studying his ledger book for this year 1998 brought the word antiquated to mind. A successful business run like this. Standing ovation for James Duffy.

One afternoon I arrived and found Mr. Duffy gone. As usual, I settled down and soon the hard hats trickled in and out, door slamming harder than before and a lot of cursing between them. Foolish me figured after a month the men were used to a female in the office.

A short tubby guy, Matt said, "I need a miter box fast." I didn't know what a miter box was or where one might be.

"Sorry. Can't help you. Mr. Duffy should be back soon." Hmm. More to learn.

Then Larry, one of the worst hecklers, came in, perched his dirty coverall butt on my clean desk and asked for a rasp.

"A what?"

"A rasp."

This time I thought I had a better answer. "Just ran out of them. Borrow one if you need it right now."

He said to the men crowding in, "See, I told you. She don't know nothin'."

They were making fun of me. I worked on, wondered if the act had something to do with me all alone for now. All of a sudden, one of the guys stomped in, grabbed me by the arm, jammed a hard hat on my head yelling, "Charlie, we need you to move the . . ." and we were out the door.

A tall yellow backhoe idled outside the trailer, no driver in sight. I climbed way up, slid in behind the wheel and checked it out. I had experience driving big trucks before, a bulldozer, tractors. This baby needed all my brainpower to figure out. Below stood the men, smirks on five o'clock shadowed faces waiting for me to cry or spin out. Instead I shifted gears, and said, "Where do you want it?"

He pointed, I drove, loved the way-up-high seat, higher than any truck I'd driven back home as a kid. Loved the power. *Look at me, Chicago.* I knew they tested me, these hard working men so much like union workers I'd known in the past. Maybe this time I passed the test.

I dismounted like a gymnast with arms up to the sky.

From then on, I became one of the guys. So I thought.

Thanksgiving holiday, Shelley and I rode the train south to Lake Shore Drive. In our many conversations, I never mentioned the kind of home I lived in so when Edgar opened the door, Edgar the butler dressed in his black suit, I heard a quick intake of her breath. As for Edgar, on seeing my beautiful, tall enough to look him right in the eye, black roommate, he also caught his breath.

After hugging him, I said, "This is Shelley Jackson, my roommate."

He nodded. "Yes, she is."

"Where is everyone?"

"Mr. and Mrs. will be home shortly. When last seen, Lord and Lady were outside in the doghouse. Robert is sniffing in the kitchen where Ms. Appleton works to prepare the ongoing feast. Sean scrubs the basement in preparation for your return."

"Thanks, Edgar."

"Roger and out." He disappeared into the dining room or garden room. I never did find out where he went.

Shelley inclined her head to whisper in my ear. "Does he always talk that way?"

"What way?" I ran up the curving stairs happy to be home.

At the top I turned to find Shelley taking her time, one hand trailing along the polished wood railing, head moving back and forth taking in the sights; paintings on the walls, sculptured pieces, thick carpeting.

When she reached me, she shook her head as if to say 'I thought we knew each other so well but this is a surprise.'

I grinned. "Follow me."

We entered my suite. New draperies and a bedspread in shades of purple, lavender, and white had been added to the décor plus a daybed for my guest. Spider plants in white wicker baskets hung from the ceiling. Even the dog beds were purple. My pups had grown so big, they needed their own large spaces to sleep.

Speechless for once, Shelley unpacked and sat.

"What?" I said.

"You might have warned me, Charlie. I thought you were just a scholarship student like me, smart—a jock without funds."

I flopped back on my bed. "Back home, I came from nothing. Worked jobs, plural, since I was a kid, to help out. I had no idea what kind of place Mom was sending me to until I walked up to the door, rang the bell and saw Edgar." I sat up. "This is the best thing ever to happen to me. My aunt and uncle took me in without a word and I try not to look back. So let's enjoy every minute."

A change happened right then. My roommate took on an aura of a mature person far beyond her eighteen years. Thoughtful and patient like the doctor who made house calls to our shabby apartment in Minnesota, she said, "There's more to your story but thanks for telling me this much."

Someday, with her uncanny insight, Shelley will be a great psychiatrist.

"Come on. I want you to meet my dogs."

The spell broken, we returned to being girls on a holiday out for fun.

At dinner, Uncle and Aunt welcomed my friend with obvious pleasure. Acting the way I thought doting parents would, they were relieved to find Shelley articulate and bright, willing to reveal her background in Alabama. I learned more about her over a meal than in the months of living together.

Instead of Robert serving and making his presence scarce, he faded into the woodwork and remained in the room to listen to the conversation. Edgar also found excuses to hover. I got a huge kick out of observing the reaction to Shelley who, poised and composed, conducted herself in a lady like fashion. Not at all the wonder woman who pranced around our room naked all the time.

Over chicken broth with slivers of chicken, rice and scallions, Uncle said, "Where are you from, Shelley?"

"Mobile, Alabama."

"Ah. We passed through on our way from Pensacola to New Orleans a long time ago. A lovely town. We didn't have time to take the recommended tour of beautiful old homes "

RECONSTRUCTING CHARLIE

Soup finished, Shelley placed her spoon in the bowl, hands folded in her lap.

"Mr. Alfred, we didn't live in a lovely part of town. My grandmother worked over there, cleaning beautiful old homes to give me advantages other girls in our part of Mobile didn't have." She grinned at me across the table, her dark skin reflecting the candlelight. "Now Charlie and I are friends and I'm so pleased to share this time with family she refers to as her faves in the whole world."

I couldn't stop the giggles. Big smiles all around and Robert collected empty bowls. Salmon to be served next. I could tell from the mesh covered lemons in a serving dish.

Half way through the elegant meal, Aunt Eleanor said, "I'm interested in your basketball background. It seems a natural sport for you with your height but where did you learn to play?"

In a matter of fact tone, Shelley said, "Have you ever watched a television show where a bunch of sweaty black kids play basketball on a broken down court?"

Aunt thought about the question. Uncle nodded and said, "Yes. We have and in some movies."

"Then you have the answer. I grew up with boys like that. Boys with nothing to do but play ball, do drugs and drink. Because I'm tall, they let me in the games. Nothing fancy but they could move and I learned. Never told Grandmother, though. She made sure I toed the line. In high school, the gym teacher paid attention, polished my game, and I became a stand out." She sipped white wine served in crystal. "A modeling agency contacted me. I turned them down. Like Charlie, I have a long range plan."

We walked Lord and Lady north on Lake Shore Drive in the dark chilly night and marveled how alike we were. I didn't think my roommate had ever killed anyone, but maybe she'd thought about it once or twice while she battled the evil boys on the broken basketball court.

Chapter 20

The big countdown before Christmas break came right after Thanksgiving. Study for tests, nap breaks, and endless pressure as I worked at Duffy's after school. Mr. Duffy agreed to keep me on and pay slave wages. I planned to insist on a raise soon. The men accepted me as a fixture and I moved closer to understanding the business end of construction.

The current project—a high rise condominium with exercise facility, pool, and you name it, had an opening for summer 1999. How Mr. Duffy expected to accomplish this baffled me with winter coming on yet his reputation spoke for itself. He always brought the job in on time, the men said.

When the boss saw me on the backhoe one afternoon, he yelled, "Get the hell off."

I finished digging the hole, cleared the dirt, rocks, and junk and parked.

"She's better than Max," Mike, the foreman said. "Much better."

"Wipe the shit-eating grin off your face, Costigan," Mr. Duffy said and stalked back to the trailer. "If anyone asks, say she's twenty one."

Without meaning to, Mr. Duffy taught me to read blueprints. I learned by observation. Later I checked the blueprints, made sure so far everything looked the way the architect drew it, and saw my future. Somehow, I'd manage to study architecture and law—not as majors, just to know. Having a photographic memory was a major plus. I also must have a feel for the work.

A sign –up sheet posted on the work schedule board alerted me about the annual Christmas party Mr. Duffy gave for the crew. Already all the guys had signed their names.

I said, "Mr. Duffy, am I considered to be part of the company now?" and handed him a cup of hot chocolate and a donut. *How could he say no?*

He knew me by now, knew I angled for an invitation. "Oh, I guess. You've done a good job. Set me on the straight and narrow but Charlie, when your cross country starts up again, who's gonna fill your shoes?"

"I promise I'll find someone to fill in. Athletics and academics got me the scholarship and my uncle said if I didn't get all A's, I couldn't work here."

Peering over his glasses, he gave me a serious stare. "Sounds like good advice. Who's your uncle?"

"Stuart Alfred. He's a lawyer."

A broad smile creased his worn face. "Saints be praised. Old Stu's niece is me office manager. Give me his phone number, Charlie." He pounded the desk looking happier than I'd ever seen him.

When I locked my computer in a storage cabinet and packed to leave, Mr. Duffy said, "Bring a date."

Laughing, I walked out into the cold dark night. A date? I didn't date. Too busy, didn't know any guys well enough to like them. A picture of Tom Donnelly crossed my mind. We had one class together. Spanish, language requirement. Again as in high school, we sat next to each other; again we never spoke to each other. I'd seen him in the dining hall talking to blond girls with straight hair wearing cashmere. I also remembered well how he had his football team members take turns watching over me. It didn't make sense. Determination kicked in. He would be my date to the Duffy party.

Fate stepped in when Shelley told me Pat planned a New Year's Eve party at his apartment and he wanted Tom to bring me.

"Hmm, I wonder what Tom will say to that?"

Shelley grinned. "Pat is Tom's idol. He listens and follows advice. My question is do you want to be with Tom?"

"We're talking date here, right?"

"Yeah. I'm not talking about moving in, wedding vows and the like. Just an evening out for fun with a guy. Something you never do."

After preparation for the next day, I snuggled under my quilt. Shelley did her nightly routine stretches and settled in bed.

In the darkened room, I said, "Mr. Duffy's having a party for the company and told me to bring a date. I considered asking Tom. Coincidence, huh?"

In a sleepy voice, my psychiatrist-to-be roommate said, "There is no such thing as coincidence."

The next day, I asked Tom to the party. A slow grin touched his lips and lit up blue eyes I'd connected with across an applauding crowd at graduation last June.

"Sure," he said. "Love to," he said. "When?" he said.

On a bitter cold Saturday night three weeks later, Tom knocked on my door. Dressed in one of Shelley's many hot −not too hot, I'd warned her, no cleavage—dresses, this one in a shiny fabric, burgundy high neck with long sleeves, too short flared skirt. She stalked around me a bunch of times before adding a wide hip hugger belt with rhinestones. I brushed my wavy hair and thought I looked just right. She grabbed some pins, pulled my hair way up, fastened the do and dropped a few random strands around my face.

"Take a look."

Transformed by the latest fashion complete with hair do, I said, "Wow! I love me. Thanks."

When Tom knocked, I'd just pulled on new high black boots.

And there we were face to face, no books, desks, or other students between us.

"Hey, right on time. Welcome to home away from home. Meet Shelley Jackson, my roommate." I blithered along all the while wanting to take a bite from the deliciousness of him.

He stepped back as if he'd knocked at the wrong door and wondered where Charlie Costigan had gone.

I turned to Shelley to ask if the outfit we'd put together a minute ago still looked terrific. She grinned and gestured for me to make a move.

Waving my hand in front of his face, I said, "Earth to Thomas. Come in please."

He blinked. "It's you," and pulled me into his arms for a hug. Not too close. Not with my stiff arms hanging down.

Somewhere a camera whirred, snap, snap, heat clicked on in the room, more snapping of pictures and Tom pulled back for another look. "It's really you."

Shelley said, "It's been interesting, Tom. Take a coat, Charlie. Good night."

Tom reached for my hand when we reached the street. A first for me. Of course Tom didn't know much about the virginal me and he might not be thrilled when he found out. My hand felt comfortable in his as we walked four blocks to the Italian Ristorante in Evanston, the party in full swing when we arrived. A jukebox in the corner played Ella Fitzgerald singing Too Darn Hot, an old song Mom loved. *Mom in Utah so far, far away.* My feet itched to dance or at least to start tapping a toe. I found Mr. Duffy with his wife and introduced Tom.

He said, "Thomas Donnelly. Are you Kevin Donnelly's boy, the cop?"

"No sir. The detective in the family is my brother Patrick."

Small town, Chicago.

We visited with the Duffy's. Tom had a gift for small talk, something else I needed to learn. Mrs. Duffy, an upscale well-dressed woman, made reference to Aunt and Uncle.

"Yes," I said. "I'm their niece. Uncle Stuart told me he knew both of you when I told him I worked at Duffy Construction."

Another couple waited for their turn at the Duffy table. I thanked the boss for inviting me along with my guest. My chest expanded with a deep breath when the two of us moved along. Thomas Donnelly from a well-known family, easy in his own skin with me, the nobody from nowhere who wound up on a doorstep. *Become somebody, Charlie.*

Tom and I checked out the endless variety at the buffet table before making selections. He pointed to antipasto, I admired the risotto with vegetables. Further down the line were pastries. I elbowed him in the ribs.

"Mmm. Looks fine. Let's begin with dessert and work our way back to the main course. What do you think?"

He whispered in my ear sending tingles down my body. "Don't elbow me in the ribs again. It's called a penalty. As for dessert first, I agree just this once. Next time, I choose the order."

Next time. He said next time. Are we having fun or what?

One tray for us; cannoli, tiramisu, biscotti. We found a table and shared.

Mike Connor, the main man under Mr. Duffy who gave me a hard time at first and now treated me much better, made a beeline for our table.

"Hi Charlie, this is Angie, my wife. She wanted to meet you."

Tom, ever the gentleman, stood up to say hello and shake hands. "Tom Donnelly."

Angie slid into the chair next to me, her heavily made up eyes giving me the once over twice. Serious scrutiny. I didn't like it but smiled and tried to think of what to say.

"So Mike tells me you're the new office manager," she said with those scary eyes narrowed.

"Yes, I am," pleased to hear Mike talked about me as office staff.

"And he said you can drive a backhoe like a pro."

Tom raised his eyebrows. I shrugged. "I've got a lot to learn."

"Huh," she said. Mike dragged her away.

"You drive a backhoe?" He scooped the last piece of cannoli and fed it to me. "You're like a diamond I've just uncovered. There are many facets to you, Charlie and I intend to polish each one."

For a moment, in the midst of this noisy crowded party, there were just the two of us.

I looked away first, afraid of the feelings he stirred in me. "Tom, where did you learn to speak like that?"

"You inspire me."

Was this a line? "I don't have experience dating, Tom. Please don't say anything you don't mean. No bullshit."

Appearances might be deceiving but as I searched his clear blue eyes, the shape of his face with wide cheekbones, and the neatness of him, I believed he told the truth when he said, "I promise."

"Let's try the main course now but first, the ladies room. Be right back."

He rose when I left the way I'd seen Uncle Stuart do many times. A gentleman.

Someone came in close behind me when I entered the ladies room. I turned and when I saw Angie Connor, I smiled and said hi.

Stepping too close, invading my space, she said, "Stay away from my Mike. You're just a kid and he's a married man. My man. Got it?"

I could have knocked her flat on her ass. What the hell?

Moving away from her, I said, "Angie, I don't know what you're talking about. I work there. That's it. Mike's all yours. Stay out of my face."

A few minutes later I heard the door close. Shaken, I went back to Tom. He knew from the look on my face something had happened. I told him about the brief exchange word for word including my inner thoughts.

He warmed my cold hands. "Her husband made the mistake of telling her about your prowess with the computer and the other side of you that makes you one of the guys. Then she meets this gorgeous awesome young woman and feels shabby by comparison. Jealousy is a devil."

"Gorgeous, awesome?"

"Yes. Don't forget diamond with facets to be polished. I'm sure there are more attributes. We haven't known each other long enough for me to find out."

"Let's have the main course now." I said.

"Well, okay."

At my door, Thomas Donnelly kissed me for the very first time. Then we kissed each other.

"Patrick is having a party New Year's Eve. I'd love to welcome1999 with you."

"Me, too." I said.

And so it began. My first romance.

The Dining Hall, once inhabited by bright eyed students now held tables of slack-jawed zombies, chins propped up with one hand while eating, the other hand turning pages in heavy text books. Just before winter break came the big push. Tests and more tests after hours of studying.

Waking up the last day I thrilled knowing I'd done well in all classes, A across the board. Shelley groaned and stumbled from bed.

"I'm afraid I didn't do as well as you, roomie."

Concerned, I said, "Good enough to stay on target?"

"Not sure. I'll have to check. I sure wish I had your brain."

Returning a while later, she said, "I'm all right for now but I got a warning to shape up in Psych, my best subject."

I'd made her bed and placed an apple on the pillow along with a wrapped package. "Juggling sports and academics is hard. Focus is the key. This is an early Christmas gift." She tore off the paper and said, "Oh, Charlie."

I had purchased another print of the horse with blinders on as a present for her.

"The race is on, my roommate."

Chapter 21

Edgar announced for all the house to hear, "Mr. Thomas Donnelly is here to see you, Miss Charlie." Lord and Lady were the first to overwhelm my handsome date. They wagged tails, danced around sniffing his heels to finally settle in a proper sit. Teetering on silly high silver heels, I clung to the banister, my long black velvet dress, slit almost to the hip, a threat to life and limb. *Why, oh why did I ever let Aunt Eleanor and Corrine talk me into this?*

Tom have must sensed my descent from the heavens above and turned his attention from the dogs to me. I admired him from half way down and knew he felt the same toward me from the heat flowing up the staircase. Me—at seventeen, a rare specimen. Virgin. Thomas—eighteen, experienced, the golden boy. Every mother's dream for her daughter.

By the time I reached the bottom stair, Uncle Stuart and Aunt Eleanor met my date for New Year's Eve, exchanged pleasantries and to my surprise, had a camera ready to capture the occasion.

"Charlie," Tom said, kissing my cheek, "you are gorgeous, awesome, a diamond. . ."

A flush rose to color my already made-up face. "Hi."

Uncle Stuart snapped away with the latest equipment and let us go with Happy New Year blessings. Aunt squeezed my hand, said she loved me and turned away. Edgar remained at the door silent and Robert blew a kiss. Even Sean peeked out to call another Happy New Year. The dogs barked and ran to Sean.

"Nice family," Tom said as he helped me into a shining dark blue Mercedes. "Dad loaned me his car for the night."

"You'd think I was going on a long trip instead of a night out the way they all carried on. Too funny but they are the best."

Before he turned the key in the ignition, Tom said, "What if this was a long trip you were going on. With me."

Puzzled, I said, "What do you mean?"

"We're together entering a new year. Who knows what it will bring."

"No one ever knows, Tom. You go along day to day doing your personal best and then a glitch happens. I put blinders on when I run and focus. That's all I can do to survive and succeed."

The car roared to life.

"You're tougher than I am, my love."

My love. He called me his love.

Patrick had an apartment on the near north side, first floor of a remodeled old house. Jazz spilled out of the windows onto the snow covered streets. Through sheer draperies, I caught sight of Shelley, elegant in a white spaghetti strap gown, Pat at her side, one arm around her waist. A large pine tree decorated with lights lit up the lawn. Tom parked and kissed my cheek again before opening the door.

"Sorry about the serious talk. I'm not an easy going kind of person. That's why I'm buried in text books all the time and then there's football. I'm intense about a career in law and sports helped to get me the scholarship. I owe so much to my folks and Pat. And then there's you."

Me? What do I have to do with all this? I didn't say a word yet he read me.

"I saw you in the hall with your uncle that first day at Randolph and wanted to shield you from all the mean crap that happens in any school. But I had to concentrate. Junior year was critical. So I appointed different team mates to watch after you." He glanced at me. "Did you know it was me?"

"Well, yes Tom. Especially when one of them said 'Cap sent us' and I thought, how kind since you never, ever talked to me. Or even grunted."

So much for the serious mood.

I said, "It takes a while to get to know someone and we're just at the beginning. Each time we're together we learn something new. Like fitting puzzle pieces to make a picture, you know? So let's go to the party."

He caught my velvet covered arm and turned my face to his. "Tell me one thing about yourself before we get out of the car."

I thought for a moment and made a snap decision. "I'm a virgin and plan to stay that way until. . ." *Until what? Until hell freezes over? Until I say "I do" with the right man kneeling next to me echoing my words. Yes.* I got out of the car so fast I didn't stop to see the astonished look on his face and by the time he caught up with me, he was all smiles.

When the ball dropped in Times Square and the partygoers counted down, Tom and I were in the one quiet corner to be found. A porch at the back of the old house overlooked the yard where frozen stalks of corn never harvested, rustled in the night wind. Two vacant rocking chairs moved back and forth. Tom sat and pulled me on his lap.

He began with little kisses all over my face, neck, ears and my mouth reached for his, lips parted. His tongue tasted mine. *Somewhere deep inside, I warned myself to know when to say no. He must have majored in kissing, making out. I majored in survival skills. So different.*

"So good," he said. "You're delicious."

Slowly the rocking chair began to rock. I knew what he was thinking. His hardness against my thigh told me. My dress, high neck and long sleeves frustrated his hands when he stroked velvet instead of skin. So far, he didn't try going under my dress for easy access where I tingled and my belly hurt with desire. I prayed he wouldn't go there on his own or at best ask my permission. Let me decide. Oh Tom, I caught my breath with the yearning for him. Don't spoil us before we've begun.

Our breathing quickened, my hair-do in a mess, fell around our faces. A natural progression in 1998 or face it, kid, ever since the Pill, would be to. . . The porch door banged open.

"Happy New Year, you two." Pat and Shelley handed over two glasses of champagne. "You missed the countdown." They laughed and we were alone again.

Tom muttered, "Shit." under his breath.

Saved by the ball.

"Happy New Year, Tom."

We touched plastic party glasses. He wrinkled his nose at first sip. "I haven't acquired a taste for champagne yet." Licking his lips, he said, "I have acquired a taste for you, Charlie Costigan," and reached for me.

Resisting his pull and all it meant, I said, "I don't drink but I am thirsty and hungry. Let's check out the spread," and a fleeting picture of Max Calhoun's spread in Utah, Mom and the kids came to me. Wide open spaces, roaring open fire, toasted marshmallows, horses in a paddock. *Were they safe? Is Max really a good man?*

Not appearing to be too happy, Tom followed me back to the party.

Appetite hearty after kissing outside, happy to survive without a fight, I filled a cheery paper plate with cold cuts, potato salad and all the fixings. Tom gathered a little of this, a bit of that and didn't try to hide disappointment. Before long, he said, "Let's go. We have to talk."

Silent on the drive to Lake Shore Drive, he parked his father's shiny car and opened up. Not the door. Himself.

"This is hard for me," he said and we both began to laugh. When we stopped laughing, he said, "Remind me never to begin a trial with those words." More laughs. Holding my hands, he started again. "We both have passion for each other, right?"

I nodded.

"When a couple kisses the way we did, what's the next natural step?"

Oh no you don't. "Tom, is this a test? Come right out and say what you're thinking."

His blue eyes clouded. Maybe no other girl had resisted his charms before. "I care for you, Charlie and a man's need is to satisfy his woman and himself."

"I care for you, too. But I am not your woman. I'm my own person. I told you what I am before we walked into the party. Didn't you listen?" Shaking my head, I squeezed back tears. Too difficult, this man/woman thing and we were young.

His blond head hung down. "I guess I didn't believe you. I'm sorry. Making out's always been easy for me." He held my face with both his strong hands. "What made you the way you are? I don't want to lose you before we've had a chance to understand each other."

How much to tell? Very little.

I gathered in a deep calming breath and said, "My mother didn't say no and ran away from home, pregnant with me at sixteen. I'm seventeen with plans just like you, for a successful future. Nothing is going to stop me."

From the look on his face, Thomas Donnelly understood. If he wanted to get laid, and he did, he'd have to look somewhere else.

January 1, 1999, our short romance ended.

Three a.m. I had a key. Before I had a chance to use it, Edgar opened the door. He took one glance at my sorry face and opened his arms. I sobbed until the well of tears emptied.

"Did the son of a bitch hurt you?"

"Not the way you think. But there are a lot of ways to hurt someone." He guided me into the kitchen and heated water for tea. On my own turf, I began to feel more secure. Under the bright lights, my once sleek velvet dress appeared shabby and I could pass for a raccoon from all the crying. *Stupid girl.*

"I'll be right back," I said and left Edgar arranging a plate of pastry.

Upstairs, I shivered from my foolishness. A quick shower and shampoo washed away Tom's passion. Then I went downstairs to talk over the problem with my good friend, Edgar.

"There is nothing like hot tea to smooth you," Edgar said.

"Biscotti dipped in tea tastes delicious. You have to dip fast before it gets too soft and quick get it into your mouth," I said.

"What happened at the party?"

I told him everything. The porch, sitting on Tom's lap and kissing until we were overheated and he wanted more. How Tom said he never had a problem making out and then he met me. And most important, I'd told Tom I'm a virgin and planned to stay that way until."

"Until?"

The clock ticked away minutes of the first day of the new year as I searched for the answer in every corner of the immaculate kitchen, Aunt Eleanor and Uncle Stuart in my mind. "Until I find my true love and we are married."

"Your words were not what this young man expected to hear."

"No. Our romance is over. And you know what?"

He leaned toward me as if to catch any pearls from my young mouth. After all, I'm the smart niece Aunt and Uncle had high hopes for. "I don't give a shit."

With his straight man's face on, he said, "May I quote you, Miss Charlie?"

We did the impossible by laughing hard without making a sound.

After a quick wipe-up of the counter, we wished each other Happy New Year and said good night.

Begin Again, I wrote at the top of my notebook and fell into a deep sleep. I didn't feel the pen fall out of my fingers or my dear dogs climb on the bed. Lady's black nose must have burrowed in my neck, her pink tongue giving a few kisses before she drifted off the way she always did. And Lord with his protective ways, probably guarded the door, stalked around and finally with multiple wags of his tail, joined us with his place at the foot of the bed, in our slumber party.

Ice cold fingers grabbed me around the ankles and yanked hard dragging me closer to where he lay. Strong, oh God, so strong even though I clawed the floor he reeled me in like a prize. Then his heat, too hot for me-- just right for him and heavy breathing in my ear, my face wet with something terrible, what I feared all my life. Dear old Dad turned his face toward me, blue eyes smiling into mine, blond hair. . . "NO," I screamed. "No," I whimpered. "No," I cried.

Thomas Donnelly had invaded my night terrors.

Instead of being bombarded with questions about the party, the family wished me a Happy New Year. I guessed Edgar forewarned everyone and I appreciated the privacy. We toasted with orange juice and I handed out paper and pen to Aunt and Uncle to make resolutions.

"Resolutions? I gave up on the old tradition years ago." Uncle Stuart chuckled and set the paper aside.

"Charlie is right, Stuart. January first is a good time to reassess priorities and make adjustments."

Observing them had a ping pong effect on me. They hit the ball of ideas back and forth in their charming way and soon picked up pens and began to write. Grinning at what I'd started, I made a list. In parentheses at the top next to Begin Again I wrote: *Always remember how Aunt and Uncle are with each other. This is the picture I want to recreate someday—with the right man, all is possible. If I don't find this man, I'll be fine.*

I had a month to get back in top shape for cross country and Monday the mid-winter three week classes began. Heavy studying crammed into a few weeks and ended with credits toward graduation. I signed up for Introduction to Law, Psych 101 and Russian Literature. I knew my Russians.

"Shall we share our resolutions?" Aunt said.

"Absolutely not," Uncle said and bit into another scone.

I bet diet didn't appear on his list.

"And you, Charlie? Is there anything you want to share?"

She wants to know about last night.

"My list is titled Begin Again. Two weeks ago, I'd never had a romance, then I had one and now it's over. He wanted more than I was prepared to give." I regarded one dear concerned person and then the other. "When I picture myself happy with someone in the future, I want my life to have the give and take I've learned from you both. The immediate future is getting in the best shape for cross country and managing three winter classes beginning Monday. I can do it." I popped the last bit of scone in my mouth, dabbed at any crumbs left from the flaky crust with a napkin and breakfast ended.

No more sweets for you, Charlie. Today you begin training.

Dressed in sweats, dogs at my side, we pounded the running track at Randolph High School, a trail of cold puffs of air in our wake. Silence except for the echo of my running shoes slapping to a rhythm set by an internal beat. At my command Lord and Lady sat watchful as I sprinted once more and laughing at my own private joke, I raced up the steps to the entrance of the school, gloved fists raised in the air and danced—like Rocky.

Lounging against the limousine, Robert applauded, a wide grin on his face. He had shown up as I left the house and offered to drive. I'd planned to run in the park across the street but this turned out to be the best.

The dogs and I settled in back after a wipe down and blankets secured for them to lie on.

"Thanks, Robert. Did you go to a party last night?" I said. I knew very little about him, suspected he and Granny Apple had a thing. Didn't even know where he lived.

"We did, kind of. There's always Sean, you know. He lives with us some of the time and last night he was invited to a party with school friends. Mary made him promise not to get married and we drove him there." He glanced at me through the rearview mirror, eyes crinkled with good humor. "You've discovered more than you asked about, Charlie. Satisfied?"

So I guessed right. Smart ass, me.

"Just getting warmed up. It clears up some of my questions. For today."

Chapter 22

Bag packed, I boarded the train for the short trip to school. Shelley had gone to Alabama to visit her grandmother. We didn't get to talk after the disastrous party at Patrick's apartment and I wondered if she knew about the end before it began romance. I didn't want to spoil her whatever with Pat. Their body language lit up with a sex sign. Yes. It's great and why not? No big deal. Everyone's doing it, doing it, doing it.

Evanston. My stop. I trudged past the construction site careful not to slip on icy pavement, office lights on, Mr. Duffy at his desk. Temptation pulled me toward him. My conscious said 'get to your room and crack the books.' *Goody two shoes, Charlie.* Like Jiminy Cricket, I let my conscious be my guide.

"It's about time," Shelley said, when I opened the door to our room.

My bag dropped to the floor, surprised to see her when I thought she'd gone away and the room would be mine alone for a couple of weeks.

"Hi to you, too. What kind of a greeting is that and how come you're not with Grandmother?"

Unfolding her six foot plus frame from bed, Shelley shook her mass of curls at me. "You had a good thing going with Tom and you blew it and I'm your best friend so tell me your side."

Cross legged on the floor, we faced each other. Not what I had in mind this morning.

"There's no side to tell. Tom is used to getting what he wants and what he wanted New Year's Eve was to get laid. I told him before we got out of the car, before the party, I'm a virgin and plan to stay that way until I'm ready. He has a lot of growing up to do. That's it. Case closed."

Tears welled up in my not-so-tough friend's big brown eyes.

"You broke his heart, Charlie."

"He wanted to break my cherry."

Tears turned to laughter so loud, someone down the hall yelled for us to shut up.

"Okay," Shelley said. "Now I'm going to Mobile."

Introduction to Law. I made it in time to find a seat at the back and didn't pay attention to my ex across the narrow aisle, almost too close for comfort. A note passed to me had SORRY written in big letters. PLEASE LET'S START OVER. I turned it over, scrawled: *call me when you grow up* and handed it back.

Attendance taken, the class began. In three weeks I'd learn enough to get a taste for law. Just what I needed.

Tired of sitting, the break for lunch came just in time. The limited menu available in the Dining Hall would do. Hurrying in, I bumped trays with Jerry Kahn, a guy I'd met in computer lab at Randolph. A nerd wiz, patient with my questions, not like some of the others in class. I didn't know much more about him. Hmm. Maybe I did. He had gone to Randolph HS so he lived not too far from me; good neighborhood—no scholarship to NU, expensive school. Parents with money for their son. *He didn't have to work but what the hell. Neither did I. Neither did I. For the first time in your life you choose to work. So ask him.* A bell went off in my head. Jerry might be just the one to be a temp at Duffy's when I had cross country.

"Hey Jerry, fill your tray and let's sit together. The hall is like a tomb today."

"Sure," he said, selecting vegetable soup and Salisbury steak.

The steak looked like a fancy hamburger covered in gravy.

Over lunch, mine a chef's salad with everything in it and an apple for later, I said, "Are you interested in earning some money after classes a few days a week?"

"Doing what?"

"Some office work at a construction site close by. You'd be filling in for me during cross country season and maybe, if you like the job and Mr. Duffy thinks your work is good, something might come of it."

"You work?"

"I do." I leaned across the table. "It's part of my plan for the future. Do you have a plan?"

Jerry straightened in his chair and removed his glasses. Blinking a few times, he cleaned off a smudge I couldn't see. "Someday, I'm going have my own accounting firm. The job you're talking about sounds interesting. When do I meet the boss?"

We shared a good moment when I grinned and said soon. He wrote my phone number in a small black notebook with neat handwriting and perfect numbers. I scribbled his number on a scratch pad and promised myself to buy a little black book just like Jerry's.

Nice looking, Jerry Kahn, I thought, on the way up to my room. Not heavy, not skinny, thick black hair on the long side, brown eyes, good skin. Mr. Duffy would approve. I changed into workout clothes under sweats for the Russians.

Please don't let it be a study of Crime and Punishment. To my joy, the professor announced we'd be doing an in depth study of War and Peace, one of my all time faves, a book read several times and one I'd be thrilled to review for credit. Two hours flew by with me participating every chance I had. *Imagine me in a psychological analysis of War and Peace. Just as my early life had been a war, maybe peace lay ahead.* Mentally stimulated, I hurried to the gym.

An empty gym is spooky. Lights were on, the smell of dried sweat hung in the air, but empty with no balls bouncing, jocks around, crowds cheering, the gym didn't feel the same. The maintenance man, Mr. Schmidt called to me breaking the silence.

"What can I do for you, Charlie?"

"Hi, Mr. Schmidt. Maybe you could leave the door to the weight room open and I'll help myself, okay?"

"Oh sure. Yell when you're through. I'll be close by."

I turned on the big TV, tuned in to a soft rock station, stripped off sweats and went to work. First some stretches and the treadmill for a warm-up. I worked my legs lying on a mat lifting up and down twenty times; then clam like movement with leg bent again up and down. After the whole routine Coach had given me back in June, both legs were ready. Now weights to strengthen lower back then quads. I loved doing the lunge. I heard her voice in my head saying, "Twist your torso to work abs and hips." A glance in the mirror showed I did it right.

"Work it, baby. Work your hips." Not the coach. A male voice, two male voices. Startled, I saw two guys in the mirror enter the huge weight room. So much for being alone. Guys I didn't know swaggered by, towels around their bull size necks. Hoping Mr. Schmidt was in screaming reach, I ignored them and continued the workout. *Blinders on, Charlie.* Next came the chin-up bar where I did pull ups. The big yellow stability ball and the exercise I used it for made me think about taking it through the door and out into the wide open space of the gym. *Good plan, Charlie.* I rolled the ball out, went back to drag a mat away from the weight room, and set myself for push-ups. Focused and feeling safe in the open space, I didn't notice the giants had come hulking over.

"Now what's she doing?" one said to the other. "Beats me?" "So ask her."

Breathless, I croaked, "Go away." They didn't.

What a workout. I drained a bottle of water and collapsed. The guys sat near me, questions in their eyes.

I broke the ice. "Jackknifing to strengthen my shoulders and core. Who are you?"

"I'm Tex."

"Mac. Wrestling. And you?"

"Charlie Costigan, cross country. All the exercises are designed to strengthen the body specifically for cross country where you never know how high a hill you have to climb, what kind of fence could be in your path, and the rocks, sand, slippery grass. So you have to be fit."

"Or nuts," Tex said. "You must really like it to be here alone and it's not season yet, right?"

"Just getting ready in advance. I love every part of it. Tomorrow, I plan to run in the swimming pool."

Mac said, "She's nuts."

"Gotta go. Hey, nice meeting you." Gathering my gear, I left. The day passed so quickly and I wanted to see if Mr. Duffy was still in the office.

Friendly fun to talk for a few minutes with a couple of jocks, I found myself more relaxed in conversation. Maybe they were good guys. On the way to the office I realized most guys are nice, what you might call good people but I must be aware of one fact. All guys want sex. I read an article about it in one of the magazines

116

the other day. Deep in my warm coat, I felt for the pepper spray can and placed my finger in the spray position as I hurried through the darkened winter streets of Evanston.

Great, the light's still on in the office. My spirits lifted and I ran up the steps and opened the door. "Hi, it's me."

Mike Connor, the foreman whose wife Angie wanted to put out a hit on me, turned and said, "Hi, you. Happy New Year."

"Oh, I thought the boss might be here so I dropped by to say hello. Happy New Year to you, too."

We were alone in the office, at night. *Not good. Get out. His wife warned me to stay away from him.*

"I have to run, Mike. See you maybe tomorrow."

"I'm leaving, too. Wait a minute." The lights went out and the thump, thump of his boots headed toward me in the dark.

Fumbling for the doorknob, I twisted it open and a gust of wind banged it shut. Mike laughed and I smelled pastrami breath too close.

"Let me get the door."

I said good night and tried to escape into the dark. Mike caught my arm. "Let me give you a lift to your dorm. It's dangerous for a woman to walk alone at night. I wouldn't want Angie to do that."

"Uh, thanks, Mike. It's just a few blocks north."

Before I knew what happened, Mike Connor hustled me into his car and drove me back to campus. Pleasant, kind Mike just doing me a favor. *Tell that to his wife.*

Psych.

A popular professor judging by the filled lecture room, Denise Cantrell spoke with quiet confidence as if we were all important to her. About five foot six, long light brown hair pulled back from her pale face with an old fashioned barrette, her brown eyes were hidden behind large framed glasses. And she dressed in casual black cords, a tan turtleneck sweater and tweed jacket. I liked her at first sight.

"Let's discuss what we know about relationships between young men and women today and where this stems from." Perching at the edge of her desk, she continued. "The way we feel

117

now is the result of all the years spent surrounded by the give and take of our families."

She strode to the board and wrote: Action/reaction. Good behavior/reward. So-called bad behavior/punishment.

"The way you were brought up made the biggest impact on your life until now, for better or worse. What we can do is modify the impact. You can be better than you are."

Aunt and Uncle had Frank Sinatra's records and one of the songs Aunt Eleanor enjoyed singing was "You can be better than you are, you can be swinging on a star."

I listened, took extensive notes, and never said a word. Everyone scrambled to leave when the bell rang. Lost in thought, I didn't rush out. *"Home environment. . .the way you were brought up. . .modify the impact."* Her words ran through my mind on a loop.

"Ms. Costigan. Is something on your mind?" Professor Cantrell said.

Funny you should ask, Professor. Just murder. Yeah, I know. Self-defense but it's a secret and I'm choking on it and the only one I told is God.

If I looked her straight in the eyes right now, I'd cry. So I got busy with my backpack and stuffed myself into my coat. Made a big show of zipping this and buttoning that. "Just a little stressed right now. Thanks for asking," and high tailed toward the door and almost made a clean get away.

Her hand tapped my shoulder and she gave me a card. "If you ever want to speak privately, call me."

Touched by the generous offer, unwilling and afraid to accept help, I said, "I'm fine, thanks."

So far, night terrors hadn't followed me to college.

Shelley returned a week later, not a happy camper after time spent with her grandma.

Flinging clothes to the bed, she kicked the suitcase across the room.

"Hi. Have a good trip? Just a sec while I finish. . ."

"We broke up," she said.

My mind still wrapped around schedule planning, I didn't tune in to my roommate's words.

"You and your grandma?"

A rolled pair of socks hit me in the head. "Patrick said he's not ready for commitment and wants to see other women. Don't be surprised when he calls you for a date when you're eighteen. I didn't ask for this, Charlie." She threw herself on the bed and cried. "I guess I did, dressing hot. Too easy. That's what I am. You're the smart one—hold out—wait for Mr. Right or no one's okay, too attitude."

Oh shit. She needs me. I rubbed her back, dried swollen eyes, applied a cool wash cloth to flawless skin, followed by an application of silky lotion. *Hey, just like Aunt Eleanor.* "Dress any way you like and always remember, if the guy wants to and you don't, say no. And even if you want to, take a beat to think it over. You're a prize package, Shelley. Don't sell yourself short."

"Short? Did you call me short, you little twerp?" We had a good laugh.

"Tom gave me a note that said Sorry, let's try again."

"What was your reply?"

"Call when you grow up." Another round of giggles.

"When the going gets tough, the tough say let's eat," Shelley said.

Chapter 23

One snowy afternoon, Jerry Kahn and I, heads bent against the wind, trudged into town to meet with Mr. Duffy. Fresh donuts copped from the hall to sweeten the visit, a thermos of fresh coffee, all Jerry's idea, were stowed in his backpack. Sure enough, the boss sat hunched over his desk, pencil tucked behind one ear, a bewildered look on his whiskered face.

Snow blew in right along with us when the door opened. He waved and didn't look up. Only the aroma of fresh donuts placed before him got his attention.

"Thanks. Just what I needed."

Mr. Duffy pushed his chair back, peering at the two of us grinning, snowflakes melting on parkas, bringing gifts. After rinsing out the dregs in his favorite mug I poured coffee. A sniff of cream to make sure of freshness. It was. He drank and sighed.

Mental note: *Timing is all.*

"This is my friend, Jerry Kahn. Computer genius in the making and future CPA. He's willing to take my place while I'm busy earning my scholarship. I'll show him the system we've worked out."

Mr. Duffy snorted. "You mean your system, don't you, Charlie."

"If you say so. Save a cinnamon donut for me, please and Jerry likes coconut."

Right away, Jerry pointed out short cuts and we got to work. It beat sitting alone and when the men came in stomping snow from their boots to punch the clock, I enjoyed the surprised looks they gave to my new companion.

Mr. Duffy said we should get out soon before the snow storm got worse. He left, grumbling all the way with a few donuts wrapped to take home.

Last came Mike Connor. I watched the smile leave his rugged face when he saw I had a guy sitting next to me.

RECONSTRUCTING CHARLIE

"Hey Charlie, what are you doing here in the middle of a storm?" *No one knew I grew up in Minnesota where you never saw the ground from October 'til end of April.*

"Mike Connor, meet Jerry Kahn. He's my assistant and when my cross country season begins, Jerry will take over." They did the manly shake hands routine.

"I want to show you how far along we are in the complex. Looks great so far. Maybe tomorrow." He gave me the look that said time to go so he could lock up.

I put the computer in the cabinet and turned the key. Jerry and I zipped into our parkas and hung on for dear life to the railing because the steps were slippery. The loud slam of the office door when Mike left reverberated half a block away. No offer from Mike for a cozy drive to the campus.

"He likes you a lot, doesn't he?" Jerry said.

"Hmm. That obvious?"

"Good thing I happened to be there." Jerry's laughter muffled by his zipped way up jacket.

"Yeah. You saved me, my friend. I owe you one," I said and tried to give a friendly punch with my glove. It bounced off his puffy down-filled parka and we both had a good laugh.

When we got to campus, students were out building snowmen. We joined in the fun. At the end of all the rolling different size balls, a few snowball fights, and rolling some more, there were twenty five snowmen and snow-women all over the grounds. Some sat on the steps, others stood in the traditional pose; each one decked out with purple caps, scarves, carrot noses, fallen sticks and branches for arms. Someone passed a joint around, beer cans popped, and it turned into a kissing party of people I hadn't met before. Jerry planted a nice one right on my mouth. I saw Shelley in the arms of a tall jock. She waved and went back to kissing. Finally the spontaneous party ended. I turned back to see snow people quiet in the moonlight.

This is what it's supposed to be like when you're young. Now I know.

Alone in my room, I crept between the sheets, the comforter wrapped around me and dreamed of another time.

Struggling through heavy snow drifts, the eight year old girl hurries home to help with the new babies. Twins. Sisters.

What fun. She helps Mom and takes care of little Jimmy. Lots of work and she can do it. Mom always counts on her. She calls, "I'm home, Mom. I'm coming." No answer and no cooking smells, babies crying, where's Jimmy? She finds little brother hiding in the closet in their room sucking his thumb. They hug. She says he's a big boy--he's four and she needs help. She changes diapers. Jimmy warms bottles in the electric heater thing and they feed the baby sisters. They stop crying. She makes macaroni and cheese for Jimmy, sits him in front of the TV then looks for Mom. Curled under the covers on the bed, Mom is asleep, her pretty face not so pretty with black and blue marks. Something's wrong with her nose. Bent crooked and blood everywhere. The eight year old girl cries and dials 911.

Shelley held me in her strong arms until the tear stopped. "Have a bad dream, Charlie?"

"Hmm. Okay. Thanks." Pretending to sleep, I rolled over and lay motionless. I thought the old days were a thing of the past. Somewhere in my memory bank, I'd stored a passage about murder. "A murderer is also a thief. He robs his victim not only of immediate life but what lies ahead; the joy and sorrow life contains." Night terrors had joined me in college.

I wanted to shout, "What about me?" Robbed of childhood, I deserved a better life now.

Dear God, please hear me in my hour of need. Forgive my sins. I promise to give back in some way, every day.

A sense of wellbeing came into me. I slept a dreamless sleep.

Chapter 24

Before class the next morning, I visited the Shakespeare Garden. Some kind soul had shoveled the path but I still slogged through snow up to the top of my boots 'til I found the bench. Sunglasses protected my eyes against the reflection of a bright sunny morning to contrast with untouched white snow. Surprised by a clean round area in the middle of the bench, snow already melting at the edges, I wondered whose butt had been there before me. A crumpled yellow piece of paper lay just below where other boots left prints. I opened the paper and read the ink smudged words, 'call me when you grow up.' The note I'd written to Tom when he wanted to kiss and make up.

In the peace of Shakespeare's snow covered Garden, I closed my eyes and wished him well. The note went into the nearest wastebasket after I tore it to shreds.

When the office closed at five, Mike stopped by to lock up and asked if I'd like to see the progress on the condo.

In my enthusiasm to check it out, I said, "Yeah. I'd love to," forgetting the promise to myself not to be alone with him.

"How did you get into construction?" I said on the way up in a wood paneled elevator. "Did you go to school or what background and how. . ."

Mike grinned, his dark eyes sparkled. I guessed no one ever asked questions about what and how he accomplished so much working for a man like Mr. Duffy. He pushed the button for the top floor.

"I went to trade school part time in high school, joined the Union, kept taking classes and even management." In response to the wide-eyed look I gave him, "Yeah, management. Tough class but I did it because I wanted to be more than a worker."

The elevator door opened to the sauna/exercise and pool floor. "Framed out for now, you'll see markers everywhere for outlets, where we intend to place all the units." He gestured while we stepped with caution across a long and wide expanse that, in a few months, would be a selling tool for the showcase building.

Fresh wood shavings littered the unfinished flooring. I inhaled, found it intoxicating, the whole scene of work in progress. Unopened paint cans in a stack, long handled brushes, spray guns, tool boxes.

"Who is the architect?"

Mike frowned, his five o'clock shadow looked more like ten o'clock.

"You don't like him. Or her?"

He shook his head. "That's not it. He came in on a low bid. I told Mr. D I didn't like the guy but he got his bowels in an uproar and there you go. So we're stuck. I like someone you can trust. When he's not snooping around, I make adjustments that make sense for safety and still have integrity of the building. You know what I mean?"

"No."

Back in the elevator, he continued, all fired up. "You gotta know the land you're digging into. It's more than pouring a foundation and framing, especially a high rise. And the water table has to be considered. I studied a lot. This guy drew a good looking blueprint on paper. I need more to be sure."

Mike walked me through one floor and then we went down and out into the cold dark night. Clamping an arm around my shoulder, he guided me in his car and there we were. Friends now. I'd learned a little more about the business of construction. Deep in thought, I didn't pay attention when he turned on the ignition and the car didn't move. I did come to life when he turned my face to his, a hot look in his heavy lidded eyes.

"Charlie, I want you."

Oh Geez! Here's this nice guy I work with and his wife must have the car wired. I used my age card to stay friends and avoid a battle. Been there.

"Mike, I'm seventeen."

Shocked, he pulled back as if I'd shot him with a stun gun. "Oh. I uh, didn't know. You're so, uh, smart and in college, I thought. . ."

"You're a good man and married. Don't forget Angie, Mike." I thought for a minute and spoke my mind. "You're a smart guy and I admire the way you worked your way up. I learned a lot from you today and hope when I have more questions, we can be friends and you'll answer. Okay?"

The car moved forward. Mike said, "Seventeen?"

"Yeah."

"Okay."

Mike creeped me out and I didn't know how many showers it would take before I felt clean. *And what's with my pheromones leaving a trail for all the dogs to come sniffing?*

Tom Donnelly had a different girl on his arm every time I caught sight of him in the Dining Hall, on campus, at games. Different yet all the same. Blond long straight hair, blue eyes, skinny like paper doll cut-outs. Shelley and I named the bunch of them Muffy and had a private laugh because none of his ladies resembled Charlie Costigan. Serious jock, over achiever with a plan.

Chapter 25

1999 May

Sure enough, in May on my birthday, Patrick Donnelly called me at home in the midst of a family celebration. Edgar beckoned me to the phone.

"You have a gentleman caller, Miss Charlie," he said.

I giggled, thanked him and said, "Hello."

"Are you eighteen yet?"

Chilled to hear his voice, a reminder of the day we met, my arrival in Chicago and all that happened since, I managed to say, "Yes, Pat. This is the day."

"Can we get together for a drink?"

After clearing my throat and a signal to Shelley waiting for me in the dining room with the rest of my family, I said, "Pat, is this a joke? I won't go out with my best friend's ex."

"It's not what you think. I made a stupid mistake letting go of Shelley and now she won't see me. I thought maybe if I explained my feelings to you. . ."

"Uh, no. Be a man. Talk to her and only her. I'm not a go-between. Now it's time for me to cut the cake." I thought for a minute. "If you just happen to drive past here in about an hour, you might see us out walking the dogs." I hung up. *Now there's a possibility.*

I kept the caller a secret as I blew out nineteen candles, opened presents from loving family and friends. Yes, friends. Jerry Kahn, my right hand buddy joined the party. Sean brought a girl friend, Susan, who gave me a delicate pottery bowl she'd made. Aunt and Uncle sat back to enjoy the fun, pleasure etched in their faces. With love in the air, flowers blooming inside and all around, I turned eighteen.

RECONSTRUCTING CHARLIE

An hour later, I suggested we all walk over to the park for a while. The idea met with enthusiastic agreement from everyone, especially Lord and Lady who wagged their way into the party. My birthday. The day before Mother's Day, not too windy, sunny and sixty five degrees of perfection. I stepped out in the sunshine, shook my hair loose from the pony tail band and took a deep breath.

"It's good to be alive. Thanks for being with me today, everyone," I said.

Shelley hugged me and Jerry kissed me on the lips. The second time. The first time was the blizzard night when we built snow people on campus. *Hmm. A good kisser, Jerry.* Patrick Donnelly got out of his car and joined us as if he were part of our group. Shelley stiffened.

"What the hell is he doing here?" she whispered to me.

"Talk to him. It's between the two of you and it's a nice day so go for a walk to clear the air." Her eyes narrowed then relaxed as if to say why not? And they walked together kind of stiff at first and softened the longer they moved forward.

Jerry said, "It seems like you've maneuvered something here with Shelley and the ex-boyfriend you mentioned."

"Who me?"

"Yes, Miss Charlie."

"I like to bring the players together and watch. It's up to them to sort things out."

"Sounds like a plan."

Once in the park, I put the dogs through their obedience paces to show off their talent. Jerry's new camera whirred catching the action. Sean and Susan sat on a bench engrossed in each other. Robert had told me they each lived in group homes and met in school. I wondered if they'd marry.

Now the group had dwindled to Jerry, me, and two dogs. Picking up the pace, we hurried back to the house. I wanted to spend time with Aunt and Uncle and give some thought to my family in Utah. *Like how the hell does a mother forget about her kid and how are my fourteen year old brother and little sisters. Does anyone remember I'm the one who always cared for them until she made me run away?*

"What's wrong, Charlie?" Jerry said. "I feel you getting sad."

"Thanks for coming today," I said. "You're the best."

Again he kissed me and said, "Thanks for inviting me to this special party." I liked the way he didn't press for information.

Three kisses, but who's counting?

They were in the garden room, a Strauss waltz playing while Aunt Eleanor worked on a needlepoint pillow cover and Uncle Stuart read the papers. An idyllic scene I had to ruin by calling for a conference.

"Thank you for the party. I appreciate you making my friends so welcome. They had a great time."

He peered over his glasses and setting the paper aside, Uncle Stuart said, "Out with it, Charlie. Something is weighing on your mind."

"You mean I'm transparent."

"We see right through you, dear," Aunt Eleanor said and laid her needlepoint on the table.

Pent up for too long, my words spilled out in a rush, "Mom said she'd call and she never did. Since then I had my sixteenth birthday and graduated high school. Now I'm in college and it's my . . ."

Uncle handed me a card. "This is her phone number. Call and speak with her. We're right here with you."

"Stuart located this number through an investigator a while back, dear. We waited for you to talk about it. Of course, we had hoped she would call but she hasn't changed much."

I stared at the number. A phone call away. My chest tightened and suddenly my sweet Lady's big curly head landed on my lap, pressing down, her black eyes mournful. Lord's tail thumped, his pink tongue licking my hand to comfort. I heard Aunt Eleanor say, "Oh, Stuart." Then I picked up the phone and hit the numbers written on the card.

Three rings, four and a young man's voice said, "Hey."

"Jimmy? It's Charlie."

"Hey Charlie, how are you? Been thinkin' 'bout you most every day since, uh, long time now."

Quiet on the line. I heard breathing kind of ragged like he had something caught in his throat.

"Why'd you run off like that, Sis? Leave me alone with her and the kids? Where the fuck are you? And what do you want?"

Oh my God. My brother believes I abandoned him and Mom never told him she's the one who sent me away.

"Jimmy, please listen to me. Mom sent me away. I never would have left you and the girls just like that. Are you alone right now? Can you talk?"

"Yeah."

"I live in Chicago with Mom's sister Aunt Eleanor and Uncle Stuart. Tell me about you."

"What sister and who cares. Nothin' to tell about me."

"What's your favorite thing to do?" I heard big boots shuffling, the metallic clink of what I hoped was a soda can lid popping off.

"Uh, build. Yeah. I built the new bunkhouse after the old one burned down. And it's fireproof. I learned it in shop class. Mr. Paul, he's a cool guy, he's the teacher and he says I have a real talent but Max says I don't need talent to be a farmhand."

My heart warmed with the old give and take recalling Jimmy's little face puckered up with questions.

"That's great. I'm involved with building, too. How are Mom and the girls?"

"Max is strict with the girls but they're okay. Mom's fine. Happy. She rules the place. Just what she always wanted."

"Okay little brother, I have to go now. Take my number and call anytime." I looked at Aunt and Uncle for approval when I mouthed 'call collect'. They nodded. "And call collect."

"Collect? You sure?"

"Yup."

"Little brother?" He laughed. "I'm six foot two and growing, little sis."

I gave him my number and address. When we hung up, I had a half empty feeling.

When my voice cooperated, I said, "He's talented with construction."

"Add Jimmy Costigan to your list," Uncle Stuart said.

"What list, dear?" Aunt Eleanor said.

"Charlie's list for her future business. Am I correct in assuming Jerry Kahn is on the list?"

"You are so right, Uncle Stuart. His plan is to become an ace CPA. I do like a man with a plan."

Aunt Eleanor rose from her chair, graceful as a dancer, and placed her hand on Uncle's hand. "I too love a man with a plan. Let's take a walk through the park and then give our girl her birthday gift."

Gathering the gifts, I went upstairs to my suite to open the large heavy box from Jerry. He asked me to open it after he left, in the privacy of my room. Too big for earrings or personal uh, unwanted more stuff. All other presents had been opened at lunch. Another golden apple with a shamrock etched on the back came from Granny Apple and Robert; this one hung on a gold chain for good luck. Sean framed a picture of Mercury he'd drawn in black ink wash complete with winged strap heels. My glass filled to over flowing. I would hang it next to the horse with blinders bought the first day in Evanston last August. And Edgar, my confidante and close friend surprised me with his choice of a simple gold cross.

Time to open Jerry's gift. I shook the package wrapped in brown paper with a red satin ribbon tied around and a cockeyed bow on top, heard a rattle and tore it open. A shiny tool box with my name engraved. And inside were tools. I hugged the big tape measure, danced with my own hammer and settled on the floor to examine a set of screw drivers and an electric drill. What do you say to a guy who gives you a gift like this? *Just say thanks, how thoughtful and like that. Don't lead him on to think he's entitled to uh, more than you're willing to give.* He knew the way to my heart, this guy.

The three of us, Aunt Eleanor, Uncle Stuart and I, had a marvelous dinner out at Le Petit Auberge, where we were treated like royalty or at least like favorite customers. After filet mignon dinners all around, a sweet cart wheeled to our table and I selected crème brulee. Oh my. When I turned to admire the selections, someone dear and near had placed a black velvet pouch in front of my spoon.

"What's this?"

"Open it, dear."

RECONSTRUCTING CHARLIE

I loosened the drawstring and shook out a key. A car key. When I first knocked on their door two and a half years before, a stranger, they embraced me as if I were their own just as Mom requested in her letter. When I expressed embarrassment at having a limousine taking me to school, they said someday they'd give me a car. Then I bought a bike with my own money and forgot about a luxury like a car. When I asked how I could ever give back to them all they'd given to me, they'd said by excelling in academics and sports and then your future plans.

"For once, I'm speechless."

They beamed. "It's not new but it's yours. Whenever you want to use it. We'll drive to the garage where we've kept it waiting for you," Aunt Eleanor said.

"But where would I go? I take the train to school. There's no parking on campus that's worth spending money on."

"Oh, you'll figure it out. Spread your wings a bit when you have time, my girl," Uncle Stuart said.

Twenty minutes later Robert pulled the limousine close to the curb in a neighborhood still lit with liquor shops, deli counters, and action at coffeehouses. The Near North Side where Patrick lived and all the action appeared to be up the block. Maybe Jerry lived somewhere close. My knowledge of Chicago had been campus and home. A car would definitely open my horizon. We all got out into the cool May night, Robert included, and watched Uncle insert a key into a roll-up door. Robert lifted a handle all the way up, the door complained squeaking as it rose and he flipped a wall light switch to reveal—Tada!—a car sparkled under the light, auburn red, the color of my hair with a big purple satin bow tied to the wheel.

I knew three pair of eyes waited to see my reaction. *Oh my God. A beautiful car for me. I knew about dump trucks and backhoes, work utility wheels and didn't have a clue about this baby. Oh, the bird with wide wings spread and there it said Thunderbird. Charlie Costigan, you've come a long way.*

"Sweet. I know it's a dumb thing to say but really sweet. It's awesome and matches my hair." I slid into the front seat upholstered in the same color leather. "You said it was old but it looks new."

"1978, my girl. The car is a treasure as you are to us. Not many miles on it. Robert drives it once in a while."

"Happy Birthday, Charlie dear."

Robert locked up and handed me the key. Before you go back to school tomorrow, let's take a little ride." He grinned. "Open her up on the highway north."

"Fine! Robert. So fine."

Chapter 26

North of Chicago. A whole different experience. The landscape changed to woods, nice homes on good sized lots with swing sets and basketball hoops over garage doors. The further north we drove, the bigger the property and homes set way back where they couldn't be seen behind fences and hedges. Robert pointed this out to me as I drove. Me behind the wheel and the T-bird handled like a dream. We passed Skokie, Wilmette, Winnetka, Glencoe, Highland Park and Robert directed me to a deli in a town called Fairview.

"Mary apologizes for not making a picnic lunch. She's going with Sean to meet Susan's family," Robert said with a grin.

"Are they in love?"

"I believe so. We'll see what her family thinks about the kids getting married before they have to. Mary and I believe it's a good thing and they're in love."

On that happy note, Robert bought sandwiches and iced tea while I stretched and sniffed the air. Sweet and clean.

"There's a small park at the beach. Let's have lunch there," he said.

"You've been here before."

His eyes looked into some middle distance and a shadow crossed his face. "Yeah. I grew up here."

I wanted to say tell me, tell all, my friend but somewhere along the way I'd learned to restrain myself and wait. He'd open up and it better be soon. "Oh. The park sounds perfect. You drive now."

See Charlie, you're not the only one with secrets.

RECONSTRUCTING CHARLIE

Picnic tables placed under shade trees near Lake Michigan on a balmy day. What could be better? *If it seems too good to be true maybe it is.*

"Why are we here, Robert? Am I missing something?"

I'd caught him in mid gulp and he sputtered tea all over. Mopping up, he laughed. "You have the most direct way of speaking, Charlie." He caught his breath. "Okay. I just felt like you weren't getting out to see the countryside, always studying, running, working, and Mary and I thought a trip north would be good for you."

"That's it? No other motives?"

"Nope. Mr. and Mrs. can take you to concerts, plays, and operas but I'm the guy who can take you to a park to smell the roses. To relax.

"Huh. Well, it sure is pretty here. Unspoiled. Not over-developed."

"Now you're talking like someone in real estate development or construction."

"Yeah. Maybe I am. Let's drive a little further north and then go home. Thanks to you, I have an idea cooking for the future."

On the way home, Robert said, "You're just eighteen and you talk as if you're much older. Were you ever a kid?"

Tough question to answer. "No, I guess I never was."

Before I left home to catch the train, I began a journal of possibilities. I wrote: What if instead of building skyscrapers—my original plan—someday I built a sanctuary, a haven for mothers and children who needed protection from abusive fathers. On a temporary basis, until the mother had skills to earn a living and the father no longer a threat, counselors to help the transition and a day school, all under the same roof. Everyone working together to mend lives.

I reread What If. *Sounds like a pipe dream. Never work.* But what if? Endowed by wealthy patrons. *Why not?* I had more school ahead but it's a plan, a goal. *I can do it. Someday.* I made a list of attributes. I'm a well-known cross country runner. All A student. Good work ethic.

The key or one of the keys is to become a star athlete at NU. That's worth something. I packed the journal in my bag, said goodbye for now to Aunt and Uncle, hugged Edgar who always looked surprised when I made such a move, accepted frenzied attention from my poochies and ran for the train station, many blocks from my home.

Head almost spinning with ideas and the loving endless goodbye just now, I had to laugh. What fun to be a part of the Alfred family and to think, all I had to do was kill Dad and my mother gave me the only thing she had to give. Her sister.

Sean's drawing of Mercury hung next to the horse with blinders picture. My focus from now on. No sign of Shelley when I returned and I figured it to be a good omen. After some major sleuthing, I deducted she hadn't returned to the dorm yesterday; dry towels, bed made, room neat and now as daylight faded, I hoped she'd come back soon. Time for dinner and I didn't want to eat alone.

The Dining Hall began to fill after I sat down with a tray filled with chef salad, whole wheat toast and iced tea and an apple for later. In came Tom with his girlfriend de jour, Muffy #5.

I don't care, I said to myself and shoveled the tasteless salad down my throat, almost choking on tea.

"Hey, slow down, Charlie."

Tex, the wrestler from the gym, moved a tray filled with everything the cafeteria had to offer next to me. His choices looked a lot more appealing than what I picked. He settled his muscled self in the closest chair and gave me a big toothy smile. Then Mac, the other wrestler, flanked me with his bulked up presence and I wasn't alone. In fact I viewed it mathematically. Sitting with the two of them equaled four regular size guys. Two words for you, Tom Donnelly and it ain't Happy Birthday. Take Muffy and shove it.

They teased me about my food and I gave it right back. I'd learned to make small talk and it paid off.

"How does an athlete become well known without competing in the Olympics?" I said. "Any ideas?"

"Huh," Mac said.

"We give time to the local YMCA program to teach wrestling. Sometimes reporters come over for a human interest story," Tex said. "It's a good thing to do. Builds confidence in the little twerps when bullies wanna beat up on them. They learn some moves. Makes us feel like heroes."

"How's come you ask?" Mac said.

"Just thinking about giving back and ways to do it," I said. "You've given me some good ideas. Thanks."

"Here's another good idea, Charlie," Tex said.

I had finished dinner and stood ready to say 'see you later.' "What?"

"How 'bout going to a movie sometime?" Color rose in his cheeks as he waited for an answer.

"Tex, you're so sweet to ask but I promised myself not to date while I'm here. With the scholarship and I work a few hours every day, I need all my time for study and team." I patted his muscular back. "Thanks for asking."

"You work?" Mac said.

"Yeah."

"Where?"

"Duffy Construction in Evanston."

"Geez. Tex, Charlie must be the broad, uh, the girl they said could drive the backhoe."

I'll never live it down. Hey, it might make a promotion opportunity one day. Put it in the journal. Also talk to Coach about a giving back program to teach kids the joy of running. Get local sports stores to donate merchandise or at least shoes.

"I'm the one, guys, the broad in the hard hat." We laughed. "If I do have a couple of hours free, I'd like nothing better than to see a movie with you, Tex. Or maybe the three of us?" I started to walk away, had another question for my new friends and turned back. "Hey guys, I've been wondering where you're from. Mac, you have kind of a Hoosier sound in your voice but Tex, you're not from Texas, are you?"

They glanced at each other then looked at me. "Nope," Tex said.

"So why are you called Tex?"

Again his big face began to blush.

"Aw, go on and tell her," Mac said.

Mumbling, he said, "Textosterone."

I did a double take and had to sit down. The three of us laughed, heads turned, we laughed some more. Then I tore a piece of paper from the small notebook I always carried, wrote testosterone and slid it between the two guys.

"Yeah," Tex said, "but then I'd be called Tess and that's a girl's name."

"I'm from Gary, Indiana," Mac said.

Priceless. Nothing like laughter to keep your spirits high.

"The wandering roommate returns."

Shelley sat at her desk writing, already in her p.j.'s.

"Hmm."

"Everything okay with the man?"

"Status quo. We'll see. Right now I've got to catch up on assignments. Talk to you later."

Three hours later, we were both ready for lights out. In the dark room with the cool May breeze stirring the curtains, her melodious voice broke the silence.

"I think Pat and I have begun a see saw pattern of a relationship. Ups and downs. Too many too often and maybe it won't work in the long run. To complicate matters we have the race thing between us. Maybe I should stick to my own kind." She sighed. I listened for more. "You were right not to rush in with Tom. Maybe abstinence makes the heart grow fonder." Her breathing grew heavy and regular. She had fallen asleep.

RECONSTRUCTING CHARLIE

Smart. My roommate's smart and she'll work it through. She might like to get involved with the project I have in mind. Take her mind off Patrick and keep her priorities on a better track. Yeah.

Chapter 27

Coach Riley listened. A show of impatience as she shuffled papers on her desk changed to obvious interest when I told her my idea of giving back to the community with volunteers from the team teaching kids the joy of running.

"I could present the concept to the head of sports activities at the local Y in Evanston. With your permission, I'll ask if any of the team have time and interest to devote an hour or two a week. As for me, I'll make the time."

"Charlie, do you ever sleep, hang out, act like a regular freshman about to be sophomore?"

"Uh, no." *What else could I say? A regular person doesn't kill her father.* "But it's a great idea, Coach, and I want to make it happen. You're the one who taught me about the joy of running. And a kid can do it alone and the only equipment needed is a pair of shoes. Oh, that's another idea. Maybe a local sports store could donate shoes. Running shoes. And if the program takes off, and it will, a manufacturer can get involved for donation. Picture the publicity. NU cross country team gives time to city kids and people run everywhere. Parks, schools, street. . ."

The blare of a whistle stopped me. "I get it and it's a fine idea. Let me think about this overnight and we'll write a presentation." She walked me to the door of her small office, the walls filled with team photos, shelves holding personal trophies from past accomplishments. "You have a good heart, Charlie, and you're going to make a name for yourself here. Don't be disappointed if all the girls don't participate. Now get out and work off some of your energy. See you tomorrow."

The Shakespeare Garden welcomed me with fragrances of spring, sunshine and the unoccupied stone bench. I stretched out, closed my eyes and breathed in scents to relax peaceful and calm 'til a familiar voice close to my ear whispered.

"The sleeping beauty," Tom Donnelly said.

"Go away. I'm peaceful. Can't you see the do not disturb sign?"

His lips touched mine in a gentle kiss. I sat up bumping noses with him. "Kiss one of your Muffy's and leave me alone, Tom."

"Muffy?"

Holding my head in exasperation, I said, "I've moved on, Tom and so have you. Those blond girls who look the same are for you, right?"

"Wrong." The sun grew warmer when he sat next to me, crowding my space. "Charlie, I can't get you out of my heart no matter how many girls I'm with."

I searched his eyes for truth and couldn't find any. Not like the honesty when Jerry and I were together. Of course, Jerry and I were friends not involved romantically. I pictured Aunt and Uncle together since teens in love, sharing a life and couldn't forecast me with anyone. Not with my secret.

He held my hand in Shakespeare's Garden and we sat in the sunshine with spring fragrance all around. Two students entering sophomore year. Each one on a separate course.

Maybe the magic of the garden and the opportune moment allowed the passionate kiss. I don't know whose arms wrapped around the other first, mine or his. Our mouths parted for tongues seeking. Tentative at first, as if we'd never kissed before and then more urgent. He didn't do anything but caress my back and arms with sensual stroking and somehow in a public place, I caught fire. Our tongues started a rhythmic sucking, slow then faster. Heat spread through my body. I knew I wanted Tom closer and so much closer. "Oh." I moaned as shocks began in my most guarded private core and rocketed through me. "Oh, oh, oh Tom." *Is this what kissing him did to me? Yes, it did.* Weak and breathless, I fell against him.

"What happened?" I said.

His hands caressed my hair and damp face. "I think, my Charlie, you experienced an orgasm."

"What?"

"Hmm. I think you did. From a kiss." He whispered into my ear sending additional shudders like aftershocks through me. "Just imagine if we . . ."

Catching my breath, I shook my head with an emphatic no. "Tom. You're dangerous for me. I have a plan and I'm sticking to it. You have a plan and nothing will get in your way. I'm not going to be a cheap lay. Another uh, notch in your belt." I checked the time. "I have to get ready for work."

We stood in face-off position, me disheveled, Tom smooth and unruffled. "To ride the backhoe?" he said.

So even Tom knew about me and the big equipment. "No hard hat today." I wanted to run from him instead of strolling toward the exit as if he hadn't made my earth move just before. "Well, uh, thanks for uh. . ." And not knowing what else to do, we laughed and went our separate ways.

Shelley left a note on my desk. Gone to Mobile. Back in a week. My only confidante gone, I did what I did best. Bury another secret. Tom may never fit in my future but at least I had this experience with him. Now I understood a little better what the girls talked about in the locker room. Cringing inside, I'd hear them talk about this guy's dick and how it felt. They'd laugh and name names about their dates and doing it with so and so. I would never be free like them but now I knew what an orgasm felt like and once you had one, well you just might want a whole bunch more. *There's a price to pay, Charlie. Don't let your guard down.*

My plan came true. Coach Riley let me take over when we met with Mr. Samuel Becker, the head of the Y in downtown Evanston. His brown eyes sparkled when we walked in wearing NU track suits to talk about donating time to teach his kids the sport of real running. My enthusiasm caught fire and we shook hands.

"I'll call my contact at the Tribune. Do a big spread with pictures and an interview," Mr. Becker said.

"Charlie's in charge. This is all her idea. She wants the kids to learn the proper way to run so they won't get hurt and maybe the publicity can elicit support from a sports equipment shop in town. Good running shoes to support growing feet," Coach Riley said.

I grinned and knew my course to be right for Phase One of What IF?-long range possibilities.

A sea of kids showed up at the first meeting. Right away, I knew we'd have to separate them in age groups. Two of my teammates, Cheryl and Tammy, offered to help today. With limited time we allotted two hours a week and would recruit volunteers from other teams as time went on. After raising a younger brother and twin sisters, old skills emerged as I barked out orders, blew my new whistle, a gift from Coach, and lined up the noisy crowd. A woman from the Y took attendance taken and permission slips and I noticed a photographer walk in and set up for pictures recording the event.

"When I blow the whistle once, it means stop talking and listen. Two times means follow your leader and make it fast. We have one hour."

Tammy had the younger children, Cheryl the middle bunch and I took charge of the older kids. The weather cooperated and in a semblance of order, piled down the broad steps into the back field for stretching and running in place.

One hour flew by. The kids were herded back in with promises to see them in two days and we ran back to campus.

Pony tail bobbing, Tammy said, "This was better than I thought it would be. The children loved being with me and you know what?" Cheryl and I shrugged. "I loved them right back." This from Tammy, the girl I had yet to beat in track. A whiz from New York.

Cheryl grinned. "Hot damn, Tam. Good to hear you talk like that. Race you back to campus." Tammy came in first, again.

The Sunday paper carried the story and soon we had a sign-up sheet for volunteers. Every team supported the idea of giving back to the community. Coach had a teaching assistant keep track of notifying when volunteers were on duty at the Y. The biggest news happened when a manufacturer offered running shoes to participants in the program. They had to have a parent promise to make sure of attendance so the kid wouldn't take the sneakers and run—away.

I sat back, me the fat cat, and enjoyed watching my idea blossom. Meanwhile, my work schedule moved along. Jerry Kahn and I became close associates at Duffy's and helped the boss prepare for the big opening of the completed condominiums. Another Duffy Construction job on time.

Mike Connor asked me to do a final walk-through late one afternoon. The month of June, beginning of summer with a carpet of sod in place, yellow daffodils and pink striped petunias planted in front of foundation boxwood bushes. Big equipment had been moved to show off the property. Even the trailer looked different with sod and flowers all around. I glanced all around, proud to know I'd been a small part of this.

"Penny for your thoughts, pretty lady," Mike said in the elevator.

We hadn't been alone since the night he said, "I want you" and I said, "I'm seventeen."

"I'm so pleased to have been a small part of this beautiful construction. Some day, I want to build but there's a lot to learn before then."

"Are you eighteen yet?" Mike said.

Oh no. Why do guys keep asking me that silly question?

"Are you still married, Mike? Angie should keep you on a short leash." We laughed. "What should I be looking for?"

We walked along, Mike's flashlight pointing to everything the inspector would check tomorrow. I made mental notes. He talked about code and up to par and how his job was to make sure the work rated above par. "That's why I get the bigger bucks. Trustworthy. That's me."

"I'll keep it in mind, Mike."

Mr. Duffy trusted Mike Connor. Angie Connor didn't. Someday, I'd like Mike to be my foreman. Someday, when Mr. Duffy wants to retire and sell his business to me.

Not a pipe dream, Charlie. Not at all.

"I have a proposition for you, Charlie," Mr. Duffy said. "I'd like you to take charge of sales of the condos." Pushing up the sliding glasses, he continued. "I've read about your program over at the Y and talked to old Sam Becker. He's very impressed with you. Said you're like a snake oil salesman from the old days."

"Snake oil?"

"Yeah. You could sell ice to an Eskimo. So let's put that to good use right here. Wear a pretty dress, sell and make a big commission. What do you say?"

"How big?"

He gave a hearty snort. "You're okay. I'll give you the prospective and prices. Between you and your chum Jerry, you'll sell the whole building out. I wanna go fishing."

Me in sales? Why not.

Chapter 28

"And this is what I've been up to," I said to Aunt and Uncle when dinner ended. Robert cleared my dishes, nudged me with an elbow and moved on. He hovered a lot whenever I spent time at home.

"Phase One, you call giving back to the community?" Uncle said. "I can't wait to hear about Phase Two."

"Nor can I. Please continue, Charlie," Aunt Eleanor said. "And excuse me, didn't you say you were involved in selling condominiums for Mr. Duffy?"

"Yes. I've closed on eight units, sold thirty memberships to the health club and Jerry and I are close to another few sales. We'll be sold out before Thanksgiving."

"Well done, Charlie. Your grades are still A?" Aunt said.

"Yes and cross country personal best is better than last year."

I watched the exchange of glances between my loved ones. *Please let this kind of relationship be in my future.*

"How do you keep up with everything? I never was this active in college."

"I've learned to catnap for twenty minutes here and there. Just enough to refresh body and soul. It works for me."

Robert poured tea. Uncle had a pensive look about him. "Phase Two is an important part of my plan for the future. Remember when you gave me the keys to the Thunderbird for my birthday?" Their eyes crinkled in acknowledgement. "The next day Robert was kind enough to take me out for a trial run. We drove north along the shore through all the towns and stopped in Fairview for lunch. And all of a sudden, I had an epiphany. I pictured a sanctuary, a temporary home for families. . ."

"Let's talk in another room," Uncle said, interrupting me. "We need a change of scenery."

Two yellow love birds coo-cooed from a little perch in their white cage when Uncle opened the door to the garden room. A glorious riot of chrysanthemums in autumn colors lined the floors and windows in clay pots while in the background, autumn leaves drifted in lazy free-fall with the light wind as night fell.

"Continue, please," Uncle said.

I began again. They listened as I painted the word picture more clearly thought out since the day at the beach with Robert. "At the rate I'm going, I'll graduate in two years going to winter sessions and all the credits accrued. At my age, I'm well known in sports and academics and now in giving back. Just think where I'll be at twenty. Maybe I can find property in Fairview, someone to endow the project and. . ."

Uncle Stuart raised his hand. "May I speak?"

"Oh, sorry. I got carried away. Your turn." I gulped cold tea. Robert appeared out of nowhere and poured fresh tea in a clean china cup.

"Dear girl, you carried us away with your idea. A splendid one, to be sure. And complex. But as you like to say, a possibility. There is a major flaw. Something you've overlooked in your eagerness to fly."

I searched through my memory bank and found nothing. "What flaw, where?" as if I, the wonder kid, never made a mistake. *Wrong.*

"Charlie, when you accepted the college scholarship, it was a four year commitment to be a team player and stay at school. You have three years, not two no matter how many credits you take."

"Oh."

"Don't look so crestfallen. I suggest you use this to full advantage. At some point you may even be able to take post graduate classes adding to your vast store of knowledge." He finished his tea, made a face and set it down. "Getting back to Phase Two, let me mull this over carefully from a legal point of view and see what we can come up with. I do admire your plan. Have you given up building a skyscraper here in the city?"

"It was only silly vanity like a need to see my name in lights."

"Why a place of sanctuary?" Where did the idea stem from?"

Put up or shut up time, Charlie. I took a deep breath and told them the story of home life in Minnesota stopping just before I bashed dear old Dad's head in and ran for the bus. "And that's where the idea came from. Personal experience."

Aunt Eleanor dabbed at her eyes with an embroidered handkerchief. No tissue for my lovely aunt. By chance, she'd seen the bruises the first day I arrived but never heard the whole story of life with Dad. Uncle Stuart asked Robert for a brandy. I shut up for a while and suddenly Lord and Lady burst through the door. Edgar's fine hand had led the dogs in to lighten the mood.

Tears melted away in the presence of two fluffy Labradoodles that arrived the same day I did in 1996. Too big for laps now although they didn't know it, they wagged tails and doggy smiled, sat up, rolled over and did all the tricks I'd taught them since pup-hood.

Uncle Stuart cleared his throat. The voice of authority. Even the dogs sat up and quivered with excitement. "This is a viable plan, Charlie. I will work with you to make it come true."

On that happy note, I returned to campus.

"I leave you for a little while and you've got your finger in every pie on and off campus, girl," Shelley said.

"Just stuff. How are you and Grandma? Everything okay?" I threw my bag on the floor and my tired body on the bed.

"Yeah. I had things to think 'bout like do I really want to be in college for so many years to be a psychiatrist or maybe change to social work with a doctorate in psychiatry. Maybe that's more useful and rewarding. Gram thinks so. How 'bout you?"

"Hmm. I like it a lot." So I confided in my best and only girl friend and told her the whole Phase One and Phase Two plan and watched her beautiful face think it over and see how she might fit in.

"Count me in with the kids. Great idea. As for the other, well, once I have training and we graduate, I could be part of the counseling staff. What do you think?"

"I think you better get your ass in gear and get moving. No time to waste moping over spilled boyfriends. Take summer sessions, winter sessions, accrue all the credits you can toward graduation and focus." I stripped off my tee shirt and socks. "Oh. You've had a bunch of orgasms, haven't you?" I ran to the bathroom and locked the door.

She pounded the door. "Damn you. What are you saying?"

RECONSTRUCTING CHARLIE

I cracked up. "I had one when Tom kissed me last week. Very interesting." I turned on the shower enjoying the last laugh.

Chapter 29

2001 March

Robert suggested we go back to Fairview to look at property he'd read about in The Fairview Weekly, a local paper. In our quest for the perfect land, our travels had taken us almost to Wisconsin border towns. Uncle Stuart and I wanted to be closer in.

Brisk and cold, snow still a foot deep after a severe winter, I finally decided to pry into Robert's background. "So, my friend, you said you once lived in Fairview and I caught a sense of regret. We've known each other a long time. You remain a mystery to me and I'm almost an open book to you. How about letting me in?"

His attractive face impassive as ever, cracked. "Okay. I was a kid from a broken home. No excuse. I ran with a wild crowd, got caught stealing a car and went to jail. I won't go into details but Mr. Alfred was looking for a chauffeur and my parole officer knew him. He recommended me." The light turned red. "Ancient history, Charlie. I've made a good life with the Alfred's and the second chance they gave me. I met Mary, the love of my life and then you knocked on the door. In some ways you reminded me of myself that first day five years ago, tough and scared all at once. And look at you now." Green light. He pulled into a strip mall south of Fairview and showed me the ad.

"There's an open house today. The owner is anxious to sell since the house has been empty for several years. Big property, secluded, lots of trees.

"House? I planned to build. . ."

"Open mind, Charlie. This might be perfect for your purpose. Let's take a look."

We drove another two miles and turned right onto a long winding road plowed and sanded. The trees on both sides leaned toward each other forming a natural shelter creating a cave like feeling. Already I loved it. And then we saw the sprawling house. Old yet new. A house with a history. An elderly man with bushy gray hair leaned on a carved cane held in one gnarled fist. Framed by one of the carved double doors, he greeted us. My first impulse was to rush up the stone steps and cover his frail shoulders with my jacket.

"Welcome. Thank you for making the journey," he said in a voice rusty with age as if he didn't speak very often.

We stamped snow off our boots and entered Phase Two of my plan of possibilities.

Mr. Byron offered to make tea while Robert and I had a look around. He probably thought we were a couple in search of a secluded home. Uncle Stuart said to be up front with property owners before making an offer. He also said not to say anything until I spoke to him. *Upfront? Sincere? I guessed I could fake it.*

The wide entrance had flagstone flooring. I bent to touch it. Real flagstone worn smooth from years of wear. *How cool is this?* Sparkles of color reflected from somewhere. Robert pointed up. Exposed beams crossed the ceiling and light poured through stained glass clerestory windows. *Hmm. They must be recessed beneath the roof. Thanks to Mike, the horny foreman, for teaching me.* Planked floors stained dark. Another plus. And renovated floor to ceiling windows. We moved along to the bedrooms; five of them, all spacious and three bathrooms, a powder room off the entrance. Then we found an office, kind of dusty but big and paneled in rich walnut wood. Not thin store bought stuff.

What a house. The fireplace opened to both living and dining room and a family room with jalousie windows overlooking a garden. I tried to pinch Robert's arm and couldn't. Too muscular. He tried to pinch mine. Also too muscular. We laughed and heard the tinkle of a bell beckoning us for tea. Mr. Byron had set the table to show off a modernized kitchen. Hot steam curled from a silver tea pot set on a linen cloth with cream and sugar. Small warm pecan rolls were in a covered basket. Unmatched chipped china cups and saucers at the ready and we sat. The old gentleman waited as Robert served.

"Let us cut to the chase, my dears. You love the old homestead, of course. And you are not a couple and I'm an old man with limited time. Why did you come way up here on this cold day, pray tell."

Robert looked at me. I looked at Robert. I knew we both wished Uncle Stuart were here.

So I told Mr. Byron everything. Not my secret. Nobody knew I murdered dear old Dad except for dear old Mom. *Who didn't give a shit about me now that she had a good life on a spread in Utah.*

And then we sat in companionable silence sipping tea and eating delicious pecan rolls Mr. Byron made from scratch. He rose on shaky legs and crossed to a drawer where he shuffled through a book and pulled out a recipe.

"Claudia's recipe, bless her heart." He handed it to me, flour coated, egg stained and all. "Keep it. She would have loved you." His papery thin hand touched my cheek. A wicked look came into his blue eyes. "She's here, you know."

"Here?" I said.

"Her ashes. As mine will be. You will make sure they are scattered according to my directions." He seated himself with care. "Call the house The Haven. Sanctuary is far too grand a word for what your intentions are. In time you will need to expand the house. That is in the future. There are influential people in this town to help you regarding endowments. Take note of these names."

As I wrote Brent and Grace Anderson, The Fairview Weekly; Kirk and Carly Richards, the sun broke through the cloudy afternoon. Possibilities became closer to reality.

I gave Mr. Byron Uncle Stuart's card and said he handled money matters. We hadn't talked about dollars. I didn't know what it would cost and when I asked, Mr. Byron waved his hand as if to brush the word away.

"Mr. Byron, I'll have to give Mr. Alfred a ball park figure when I get back to the office today."

He gave me a gentle reassuring smile. "By the time you reach Lake Shore Drive, my dear, all will be resolved. Now leave and we shall meet again very soon."

"Uh Robert? What happened in there?" Silence in the car until we hit the main road back to Chicago.

"I'm not sure. When I was a bad boy, I stole that same teapot from the house and my conscience nagged me so much, I returned it. To the front door. And apologized to the pretty woman who answered the door. And I brought flowers I paid for."

"What did she say?"

"She thanked me, said she knew I'd come back and invited me in for a pecan roll just out of the oven."

"What did you do?"

"I sat at the same table, had tea but the cups weren't chipped and they all matched, and the pecan roll tasted the same as today. Delicious. I wanted to cry."

"When?"

"Today."

"Me, too."

"Do you think The Haven will really happen?"

"Yeah."

"Me, too."

We drove south for a while passing Glencoe, Wilmette, Skokie when Robert said, "I should have listened to her when I returned the tea pot."

"Why? What did she say?"

"Don't take things that aren't yours. I wouldn't be an ex-con."

"Right. And you wouldn't have met Uncle Stuart or Mary or me or wound up back in the kitchen eating the pretty lady's pecan roll."

"Yeah." He pulled up to the curb.

I thanked him and ran in to meet with Uncle.

"This calls for a celebration," Uncle Stuart said, after talking with Mr. Byron and pleased with my fledgling negotiations

"I didn't do anything. Robert and I looked around, had tea and left," I said, clueless. "I don't even know how much he's asking for this wonderful house. Wait 'til you see it."

"Charlie, he liked your honesty and wants to work with us."

"So that's all it takes to do business?"

Uncle just shook his head. "It's you, personality, directness and so much more. You will learn as time goes on." He cleared his throat. I waited for more news. "Jimmy called. He's moving here. I arranged a flight ticket and tomorrow we'll have another Costigan in our home. What do you think about that?"

My brother. Sixteen now. When I left he was eleven.

"But Uncle Stuart, it's too much for you and Aunt Eleanor. I'll move out and Jimmy can live with me." Frantic, I thought of where I might find an apartment. *Maybe at Mr. Duffy's condos.*

Aunt Eleanor walked in and heard my last words of protest. With a firm grip on my arm, she sat me down on a bench in the entrance hall where we'd first seen each other more than five years before.

"I knew this day would come. When you'd think 'oh poor aunt and uncle burdened with a niece.' And now your younger brother needs a haven, a place to grow up for a while. Big deal. Before you came, we had a quiet orderly house, no excitement, just us. And the fun Stuart and I have had and continue to have watching you blossom into womanhood is priceless. Don't take that joy away from us, Charlie Costigan." She fanned her face with one of many delicate handkerchiefs. "Oh my. I haven't expressed myself with so much passion in a while."

Uncle Stuart raised an eyebrow. "Really?" She blushed. "How soon you forget."

They were flirting. Oh my god.

"Jimmy arrives tomorrow. He can have your old bedroom. From what you've said, Jimmy might like an advanced shop program," Uncle said and beckoned Aunt to follow him.

Edgar removed my coat. "Lunch is ready in the kitchen, Ms. Charlie."

Five years gone by and I knew it had to be him by the color of his hair. Auburn. Same color as mine. Long, lean and lanky best described Jimmy. The girls at the high school would cream over the cowboy with his slow drawl and easy way. And he had muscles that wouldn't quit. Broad shoulders. My baby brother. He loped along the crowded walkway, bag slung over his shoulder, weathered leather jacket open to reveal a denim shirt with snaps and a cowboy string tie, big silver buckle on a leather belt hung low on a narrow waist and worn jeans with scuffed boots.

"Hey," he said and swung me around like a feather. We had one of those moments of serious hazel eye searching. He blinked first and I squeezed him hard. "My saddle's in baggage claim. I smuggled it out when old Max and eagle eye Mom weren't lookin'."

"Hey, little bro. So good to see you."

157

Holding me at arm's length, Jimmy checked me out as if I were a horse he thought about buying. If he tried to open my mouth for teeth inspection, I'd bite. "You grew up real tasty, Sis."

"Let's go. The family's waiting for you."

When the limousine pulled up, Jimmy gave low whistle. "Get in, kid. Traffic," Robert said.

What a sweet time watching the expression on Jimmy's face with heavy traffic at O'Hare Airport, big buildings downtown, and then Lake Shore Drive, a far cry from a spread in Utah mucking stables under the thumbs of Mom and Max.

"Not too many horses so far," Jimmy said.

"You'll be surprised. There's a lot of everything here, brother. This is Chicago," I said.

Edgar opened the doors to greet us, Lord and Lady frantic with excitement yet always obedient, quivered next to him in sit/stay position

"Ponies," Jimmy said. "You have ponies in your house. This is the best." He hunkered down between them, a hand on each. Their shining black eyes waited for my command. I gave a down signal. They obeyed. And Jimmy joined the family, rough-housing with the dogs in the beautiful entrance hall the minute he arrived.

Before dinner, I had a little heart to heart with my brother about table manners, speech and whatever I could cram into his dear countrified head before I left for school.

"Jimmy, when I came here, I knew nothing about table behavior, what spoon to use and just plain old being polite." His eyes wandered around the comfortable room. I grabbed his square jaw, felt whiskers in need of a shave and forced him to pay attention. "This is important so pay attention. We don't curse here and we are polite. Aunt Eleanor and Uncle Stuart are the best friends you and I will ever have. So are the other people who work here. Edgar, Robert, Granny Apple the chef, and Sean who is a handyman and does laundry. Sean also takes care of Lord and Lady. Got it?"

"Yup. I do believe I hear you, sister."

"I plan to have a construction company someday and I need you."

"Me?"

"Yup. Sure do. So you'll go to an advanced program in shop, learn everything you can about building and design and when I graduate in three years, we are in business, brother. Deal?"

"Deal."

A knock on the door, Edgar's solemn voice announced, "Dinner is served, Ms. Charlie and Jimmy."

Jimmy whispered, "Holy shit, does he always talk like that?"

"Like what?" I said, "And don't curse."

Steak and potatoes on the menu, in honor of the young cowboy, with vegetable soup and apple pie for dessert. Jimmy kept an eye on my cutlery selection before picking up his and the meal went well. Robert moved swiftly before Jimmy made an awkward attempt to clear the table.

Uncle Stuart beamed at his growing flock. "Jimmy, tomorrow we'll meet with the principal of Randolph High School and see where you fit in. What interests you? Any sports by chance?"

With a tilt of his head, too long mane of hair swinging, Jimmy said, "Sir, I can bust broncos, rope a stir, won a rope twirling contest, ride anythin' on four legs. . ."

"Ride?"

"Yup." A stern glance from me and he said, "Yes, Sir." "Ride, jump over fences, do most anythin' on a horse. Just turn me loose. And Sir, I can build whatever you need. Got the best grades in shop. Mr. Paul says I have a real talent." Jimmy bent over the apple pie and scraped the plate. "Delicious," he said. "Oh, I swim. Fast. Had to or Mom woulda tanned my hide."

I glanced at Aunt Eleanor who appeared to be spellbound by this nephew from another planet. She hardly touched the hearty meal. I hoped Jimmy told the truth about his accomplishments. Uncle would find out soon enough. The thought of Mom's threats sickened me. If I ever had children, tender loving care is what they'd know.

"Tomorrow we'll know more about placement, Jimmy. Don't you worry. There is a place for you to shine."

The train ride back to Evanston with a mind overly concerned about my loose cannon of a brother gave me a

159

headache. I stopped at the drugstore for aspirin and bumped into Jerry. He knew my brother had arrived.

"What's wrong?"

"Headache."

"Brother worries?"

"Yup. Oh no. I mean yes."

He scooped up a bottle, ran to the counter, paid and hand in comforting hand, walked me to my room. Once there, Jerry warmed a glass of milk, added chocolate syrup, stirred and handed me two aspirins. "Drink." Removing my sneakers, he helped me lie down and covered me up. "Stay," he said. We grinned at each other in a comfortable way and I dozed to wake up two hours later, Jerry on the floor next to me.

"Thanks."

Polishing his glasses, the same invisible speck no one else saw, "Your brother will be fine. If he's anything like you, better than fine is my guess. Focus, dearest Charlie. We have a wonderful life ahead."

He called me dearest, said we'd have a wonderful life. Maybe Jerry's the one. Right under my nose. Hmm.

Chapter 30

Uncle Stuart waved his legal magic wand to make all the arrangements and Mr. Byron's property became ours. Every spare moment from then on had to be spent getting the place in shape. Robert took charge of cleaning crews inside and landscape work. Jimmy, doing remarkably well at Randolph on the swim team and in shop helped in every capacity when he didn't have swim meets. A family affair. In the home stretch for graduation, I pushed myself to the limit and then pushed some more.

A quiet moment early morning, I sat alone on the stone bench in a reflective mood. Journal open, I wrote about the me in 1996 and how far I'd come using the short story format I'd learned along the way. Rereading, I recognized a growth in expression. I had matured from a kid's perspective using slang expressions to an educated woman capable of writing and painting word pictures. Someday soon I'd stop by to thank Professor Jen Margolis and all the incredible teachers who helped shape me during the past four years.

One Saturday afternoon in late Spring, perched high on the backhoe, I peered down at an unfamiliar car approaching. With no one around, I wondered what to do. My private property and a stranger dared to approach. A tall elegant man got out of a black Mercedes, went around to the other side and opened the passenger door. Hand extended to the person inside, he kissed the trim attractive woman as she came out. Very romantic.

"Hi." I called down. "Who are you? This is private property."

A rich baritone voice called back. "We're looking for Charlie Costigan. Is he here?"

"Who wants to know?"

"Kirk and Carly Richards. He will want to meet us."

Huh. Richards. One of the contact names Mr. Byron gave me.

"Be right there." I did my usual drop down, spin around, tada flashy come down and pulled off the hard hat, my hair a mess after being squashed too long.

Pulling off work gloves, I offered a hand. He shook it. "Charlie Costigan. Mr. Byron asked me to contact you but we've been so busy cleaning up the place."

"Meet Carly, my wife." His ordinary words had a holy quality to them. "This property, the house and gardens are very special. Mr. Byron was an extraordinary gentleman."

"Was?" A pain shot through my heart. The elderly man said he had limited time and now he was gone.

"He requested that you spread his ashes in the garden, around the house and on the path." Carly Richards handed an urn to me. She looked at me with so much understanding, I had the feeling we were old friends. "I blessed them already," Kirk Richards said.

Without another word, the three of us stepped across the path and made our way around to the back. A gust of wind swept through the trees. Every branch swayed, daffodils bobbed their yellow heads, an empty sprinkling can tumbled off the brick stoop. In the gazebo two faded wicker rocking chairs I couldn't part with, didn't move. I believed they had significance to the Byron house. They remained still despite the wind, the old fashioned rockers resembling a painting someone forgot to bring inside. The Doldrums flashed from my memory bank. 'The Doldrums is the region of calm winds, centered slightly north of the equator and between the two belts of trade winds, which meet there and neutralize each other.' In nautical terms, the rocking chairs were becalmed and unable to progress. Lifting the lid, I scattered ashes close to them and suddenly they moved together, rocking in harmony as if the moment they waited for had finally come.

Transfixed at what I'd just seen, I wondered if my visitors caught the same sight or did I lose my senses for a minute. When I turned to see Kirk and Carly, I knew from the look on their faces we shared this brief glimpse into an unknown world.

"Tea, anyone?" I said.

"Perfect. We want to discuss an endowment plan for The Haven," Carly said. "Friends of ours, Brent and Grace Anderson are just the people to interest in such a fine project."

While I boiled water, my best effort at cooking these days, they explored the house. I wished for delicacies to serve but no.

Supplies all gone after the guys cleaned me out so tea and peanut butter and jelly on crackers would have to do. Definitely not prepared like a Girl Scout or Granny Apple.

"Beautiful." Carly said. "I've always wondered what the old place looked like. You'll need new furniture, of course."

Kirk got right down to business. "Lay it out for me. Exactly what you plan to do."

"Okay. Dig in to the feast and I'll fill you in."

Kirk said, "I'll be Mother," and poured tea.

I must have looked puzzled at the expression because Carly said, "Kirk was a Jesuit priest. "I still didn't get it but moved on with a detailed explanation beginning with Phase One and teaching kids the joy of running and the big finish with purchasing the house.

"I have a tentative line-up for kitchen staff, social worker, tutors. What's missing is the key of how to find the first family in need of a temporary haven. The house is big enough for one family but when we take off, and we will," I paused to catch my breath and glanced at their smiling faces, "we'll need to build an addition. My brother's a whiz with design and I have a construction crew."

"How old are you?" Carly said.

"That question is politically incorrect. How old are you?"

"Oh my. Sorry. I was a homemaker for many years before becoming a journalist. Politically incorrect is not a natural action for me."

Kirk poured more tea. "I know how to find your first family once you're ready."

I jumped from my chair and ran around the table to hug him. "How, where, when, why?"

Carly laughed. "You sound like a reporter."

"I graduate in another month so let's get a move on. When can we meet again? I'll bring my team, you bring yours."

We exchanged phone numbers and the interesting Kirk said he'd begin a search. When I asked for specifics, he flashed a mysterious smile.

"I have my ways," Kirk said and the meeting ended on a high note.

RECONSTRUCTING CHARLIE

Another urn, dusty with age and worn by the elements, lay on its side in a corner of the gazebo. I wrapped the two urns in a big old towel and carried them to where the garden hose coiled ready for use. Careful washing with a soft brush restored some luster to the urns. They shone in flickering shades of light and dark when I returned them to their proper place in the gazebo as the rocking chairs moved back and forth with a slow pace.

I thought about the way Kirk and Carly Richards were together, harmonious and unified and wondered how long they'd been married. So far, Aunt and Uncle had the special glow and now Kirk and Carly. My personal Phase Three. With Jerry, I think.

Chapter 31

June 2002

The week before graduation and all through the cramped office, everyone had gone home to barbeque, or see a ball game, or get up to no good. A popular pastime according to the men, single and married. Jerry shut down his computer, reached over and did the same to mine.

"Enough with the work already," he said and gave me his endearing grin that spoke volumes. He asked for so little.

"Come here, sweet man o' mine." I crooked a finger in his direction and walked to the little couch, threw two pillows on the floor and said, "Sit." Many times I'd been on the verge of telling Jerry about my background; unlocking the box buried deep in my head to let him peek in at just the top level and then I'd draw back afraid to spoil our closeness. The secret burdens became too great for me to handle this evening. We were alone and someday I believed we'd be one of those couples others envied.

"I'm going to tell you about my life before I came to Chicago. Only my aunt, uncle and Shelley know this secret past."

Without a word, Jerry listened, his expressive dark eyes showing flashes of anger and sadness. When I finished, leaving out the killing secret, Jerry said, "Charlie, everyone's life is filled with secrets. Even mine and I come from a loving family. We all have a locked box hidden away. I'm sorry yours is so awful."

His tenderness, the safety of his arms surrounded me. I knew we had a future together when Jerry didn't polish his glasses as he asked me to dinner with his parents the Friday night after graduation.

Our dorm room crowded with team and friends, spilled out into the hall and all over the stairs. The night before graduation and Shelley and I threw our first and last NU party. With Jerry glued to my side, I hugged a bunch of guys who puckered up for the big kiss and never had a chance. Happy to have my dear special man close so I didn't end up exchanging spit with anyone but him, we shared a soda. He'd learned my aversion to alcohol long before and respected it.

Coach Riley came over to our party for a short visit.

"You've come a long way from the kid jumping over fences the first time I saw you."

Filled with emotion for all this wonderful woman had done for me, I held back tears we both despised. "Thanks are a small word for what I've learned from you in four years. You're the best, Coach. If there's anything you need, please call on me." Someone clicked yet another picture and she left.

"Goodbyes are tough," Shelley said.

"Just wait 'til tomorrow." I said. "Is Patrick coming? To graduation?"

We shared a knowing glance. She shrugged. "Beats me. He'll do what he does. The important one is Grandma. She'll be here early tomorrow."

I hurried to say goodbye to The Shakespeare Garden. Eight a.m. no one around and I ran all the way. Dew covered flowers, the path, even the bench. I wandered to the end and back saying goodbye to this special place where I'd found comfort and my first orgasm. *Mustn't forget that.* Running back I crashed into Tom.

"Well, hello," he said.

"Hi. Gotta run. Had to say bye to The Garden."

I ran my personal best right into the shower and at age twenty one, prepared for the next part of my life.

Almost the best moment of Graduation day is forever memorialized in a picture taken by a photographer from the Tribune. Shelley's Grandmother, Jane Jackson from Biloxi, Mississippi sashayed across the field, dressed in a white flowered summer dress, her wide brim straw hat trimmed with a white satin bird surrounded by red poppies, the whole concoction anchored with a red satin bow tied under one of many chins. Shelley waved to the cheering basketball team and friends mouthing, "My Grandmother," as if we all didn't know.

To my surprise, I received accolades from the Mayor who took a moment in the sun and spoke of my sports achievements and academics while giving back to the community by teaching youngsters the joy of running. I knew he never walked two steps alone without a limousine. Politics. He glowed in the spotlight, a real pro and his mention of the program would bring financial support to the Y.

A day full of joy and sense of accomplishment followed by dinner at our home on Lake Shore Drive.

The purple and white striped canopy filled the manicured back lawn. The Duffy's came, my teammates dropped in to dance and dine under the stars, Uncle Stuart's law firm associates showed up. Aunt Eleanor flitted around like a butterfly greeting everyone while I hung back watching. *A party to honor me with Aunt and Uncle's friends, my pals, half the city appeared to be here. And why? All I did was run fast and get A's. And commit murder.* My insides began to shrink.

I smelled his familiar scent and felt Jimmy close by. His arm went around my shoulder.

"What's up, Sis? Old shit?"

"Watch your mouth, little bro."

"You done good, big Sis. Aunt and Uncle are mighty proud." He crooned soft and sweet, 'Don't stop thinkin' about tomorrow. Yesterday's gone. Yesterday's gone."

Our eyes met. "Smartass brat," I said. "How many girls did you bring to the party?" He grinned and swaggered away. We shared a different life from the one we shared now and that's a good thing. Now I joined the party ready to focus on tomorrow and prayed yesterdays were gone from my life. The next hurdle lay ahead. Dinner with The Kahn family.

A light tap at my door brought back happy memories. Aunt Eleanor hadn't come tap tapping after dark in a long time. "Come in."

Framed in the door, backlit by sconces lining the staircase, my dear aunt looked like an angel.

"It's not too late for a visit?" she said.

"We're having a pajama party and you're invited." Lady slept on, Lord lifted his shaggy head for a rub from Aunt as she pulled up a chair next to my bed. "Thanks again for the wonderful party. I loved seeing the mix of my friends and yours and the food, thanks to Granny Apple, was superb. Who ever heard of a so-called barbeque serving filet mignon with mushrooms and Béarnaise sauce and all the accoutrements I've grown accustomed to."

"Charlie, I'm aware of something troubling you. That's the purpose of my visit tonight. We need a heart to heart." She searched my face for an answer and waited, patient as ever.

Another chip in my armored heart fell away. I couldn't keep feelings hidden from my aunt. Only the dark secret. "Jerry invited me to have dinner with his parents at their home Friday night." Aunt waited for more. "Friday night. They're Jewish, Aunt Eleanor." She nodded as if say 'go on.' "And I'm not."

My aunt began with a smile, then a giggle turned into a laugh.

"What?" I said.

"I know, dear girl. I know. So?"

"So what if they don't like me or accept me?"

"We're talking about dinner right now. Not wedding plans and how to raise the children."

By now we were both laughing. The dogs jumped from my bed, ran to their own comfortable beds and burrowed in.

"I don't know what to wear."

"You're whining, dear. Let's have a wardrobe check right now and maybe then, we can all get to sleep. Stuart doesn't do well without me next to him."

"After so many years?" I said.

"Knock on wood," she said.

Opening my closet brought me back to reality. After years of sneakers, track suits, blue jeans and a few dresses for special occasions, I didn't have a wardrobe for grown-up land. In despair, I turned to see my aunt's face glowing.

"We haven't gone shopping in a long time. Now we'll look in shops where I know my way around." At the door, she turned back to give me something to think about. "And don't worry about the difference in religion. If you and Jerry are meant to be together, differences will melt away." With a click of the door in place, her scent and common sense lingered.

High boots—way high over the knee were in style. Worn with shorter hem lines, knit dresses, mannish tailored jackets, shirts buttoned low with lace camisoles underneath. Loose pleated pants worn with heels and little vests. Everything had a swagger to it. Me, the jock, didn't know where to begin. Aunt Eleanor knew every expert in all the high fashion shops. With pride, she introduced me, credits and all and I didn't mind one bit. *She's the Mom I never had so enjoy it.*

"We bought enough to get you started, Charlie. Don't worry about expense. Stuart always said you saved us a bundle with the scholarship and what you don't know is Stuart's clientele grew as your accomplishments hit the news. See, it works both ways."

With Aunt's jubilance contagious, I raced up the stairs shopping bags flying and unpacked my new wardrobe. Five years before we'd gone shopping almost like today except I no longer had external bruises to hide. My hair, newly styled, swung in long layered waves. The hunter green suit with an ivory lace camisole would be perfect for Friday night. Still not decided about the shoes, thigh high boots with high heels or black pumps with straps around the ankle and four inch heels. Hmm. *How about sneakers and track suit. Keep it simple, stupid.*

To say I made an impression on Aunt and Uncle, Robert and his beloved Mary, is an understatement. But when Edgar caught sight of me descending the stairs, he murmured, "Mama Mia." Transformed by the grace of Aunt Eleanor, I made my way down with a white knuckle grip on the railing. Deciding the high boots might chafe and be too fashionable for the evening, I wore the gorgeous lethal heels with black sheer panty hose.

Brother Jimmy came in at the same moment, yelled a Yee Haw, and broke the spell.

Chimes rang out. Aunt Eleanor shooed me back upstairs to make another entrance. Uncle Stuart cleared the hall and Edgar opened the door.

I waited for the phone in my room to ring. For dear Edgar's rich voice to announce, "Ms. Charlie. You have company." A game we played. I'd graduated from Miss Charlie to Ms. Charlie somewhere over the years.

The phone rang. "Ms. Charlie. You have company."

"Thank you, Edgar. I'll be right there." I wanted to crack up. Instead a make-up check seemed to be in order and one last lift of the hair-do. *After all, I'd done this a few moments before and who knew what might have gotten ruined since.*

Head erect since the dress rehearsal went well, I reached the bottom stair without a mishap until I looked into Jerry's eyes. Stopping to breathe and breathe a bunch more times, I gave a signal to my dear Edgar all would be fine, and stepped down.

"Hi," I said to quite possibly my future.

"Yes," Jerry Kahn said as if he read my mind.

Aunt and Uncle came out to welcome Jerry and wish us a pleasant evening. Brother Jimmy slapped Jerry on the back and said "Hey." Jimmy's face registered surprise. He didn't know how physically strong Jerry Kahn was and I did.

"You are beautiful, Charlie. Do you know it?"

We were driving west in a new car Jerry bought for himself after graduation. He signed up for the CPA exam and a lot of studying lay ahead. A planner, like me.

Jerry's saying something and all I can think of are the words THE SHIKSA COMES TO DINNER. a sequel to the movie GUESS WHO'S COMING TO DINNER. In high school we watched the movie about a white girl bringing a black boyfriend to dinner and the impact on her family. *Equality. Shelley troubled with Patrick thinking she should stick to her own kind. Even now in this century, prejudice. . .*

"Earth to Charlie. Come in please." I felt a tug at my arm.

He pulled over to the curb and parked. "What's the matter, sweetheart?"

"Jerry, what if they don't like me? I'm a shiksa."

"A what?

"You know. A shiksa. Not a Jewish woman. Your parents want you to be with someone like you."

"Charlie, I don't know where this is coming from." Off came the glasses. A sure indication of his keen mind at work reviewing the situation. "You grew up in a small town in Minnesota. Probably there were few if any Jews there."

"The banker and his family. Their kids went to private school in Minneapolis."

"So you didn't know any Jews?"

"No. But Dad always cursed the bank."

"He must have been a bigot. Did you ever meet the banker?"

"Uh huh. I saved money from jobs and didn't know where to hide it so Dad wouldn't rip me off. After school one day I went to the bank and asked the teller how to open an account. She called Mr. Goldenberg. He sat me down in a nice room and asked me how old I was." I chuckled at the memory. "Seems like people have asked me that same question forever and still do."

"How old were you then?" We laughed together.

"Eleven." We stopped laughing, me with the thought of myself as a young girl protecting hard earned money from a father. "Mr. Goldenberg poured the money out of the sock I kept it in and counted. He said I didn't have enough to open an account and scooped it back in with very fast hands and I heard him say to his secretary something like, 'Shaineh maidel.' So I grabbed the sock and ran all the way home knowing he hated me for not having enough and cursing me just like dear old Dad always did."

I sat there age twenty one dressed in fine clothes, price tags cut off a few hours before, in my dearest Jerry's new car, the fresh smell of leather so intoxicating. *Don't stop thinking about tomorrow. Yesterday's gone. Is it ever gone?*

"Shaineh maidel means beautiful girl in Yiddish, Charlie. The banker complimented a pretty girl. That's what I said when we first got in the car."

"Oh."

"I don't want to mess your make-up, well actually I do but not now, so if it's all right with you, Miss Costigan, I'll just kiss your fingertips."

The man knew his way around my fingertips with gentle lips pressed up and down and in between; one hand then the other and turning my palms up, he tasted and licked vanilla lotion right off. Body heat steamed the windows of the car as I thought of other parts he might like. He stopped. I knew we had the same idea.

The powerful engine roared, air conditioning cooled and we arrived at the Kahn home, the two of us closer than ever.

The house Jerry grew up in had huge oak trees bordering the property. An established neighborhood, most were red brick homes, two story with a basement, built fairly close together. Tidy and well cared for. He held me tight so I wouldn't stumble in the new shoes and opened the door with his key although he no longer lived there.

"We're here," he said.

The blond attractive woman hurried to greet us, a diamond Star of David nestled between her ample bosoms. She threw her arms around Jerry as if she hadn't seen him in years. "Hello, my son. And this must be your friend, Charlie. I'm Sophie Kahn, Jerry's mother."

I almost saw the wheels of her mind spinning with the first sight of Jerry's shiksa. And she all but examined the fabric of my suit checking me out. *Stop it this minute, Charlie. Relax and have fun tonight.*

"Thank you for inviting me this evening," I said.

Jerry abandoned me to search for his father. Sophie led me on a tour of the main floor complete with Oriental rugs and comfortable furniture, a Baby Grand piano and family photos on every surface. The dining room table was set for eight, candlesticks in the center flanked a napkin covered twisted bread on a platter. Aromas wafted from the kitchen making my mouth water. I wondered who else would sit at the table, where everyone hid, and where the hell did Jerry go.

"Excuse me, the soup needs one last stir and dinner is ready," Sophie said.

"May I help with anything?" I said and hoped she'd say no.

She smiled. "Just pick up that little bell, go to the stairs and ring it. Everyone will hurry down." Sophie Kahn, Jerry's mother disappeared into what I guessed was the kitchen.

Ring the bell I did and down rushed Jerry, Bernie Kahn, his dad, twin girls about ten, an older version of Jerry, must be the brother he seldom mentioned and the brother's wife. A whole family. In short order I met the pleasant father—a CPA, a quiet older brother Leonard--professor of English Lit at a private college, Elaine his wife, a middle school social studies teacher and the twins, Haley and Heidi. I fell in love with them before the evening ended.

Sophie flitted about seating everyone and then draped an ivory lace doily over her head, lit the candles and chanted in what sounded like Hebrew. A prayer, maybe to bless the bread. She waved her hands and chanted. Beautiful. When I glanced at Jerry to show how much I liked the ceremony, he had a perplexed look on his face as did everyone else at the table. Sophie ended with something like ah mein. I joined in with a white bread version, amen. The family's amen kind of staggered in after mine. I wondered what had happened when out came a wait staff person with soup and balls.

Everyone oohed and Jerry said, "Mom's matzo ball soup is the best." Again, he shrugged and enjoyed the soup.

Tasty, a bit heavy for me but I broke the ball things into small pieces and finished.

The next course was something called gefilte fish. Served on a small plate with sliced carrots, I decided to give it a pass and edged it toward Jerry. He shook his head as if to say no way, kid and there it stayed until the nice waiter cleared my plate. I wondered if Sophie took notes on how Jerry's girlfriend responded to her cooking. *Granny Apple she isn't but who is?*

Heidi and Haley knew about my cross country fame and asked me a lot of questions about how I got started and the training. Heidi said, "Grandma wants us to be dancers. "We want to be like you," Haley said. I'm sure this didn't earn me any points with the possible in-laws.

Jerry squeezed my arm and said he went to all my meets. "She's awesome, girls."

Pot roast deserved first prize. Not the best choice on a June night but I gave Sophie the blue ribbon. She basked under all the attention and sprinkled her conversation with a lot of words I didn't know. Maybe Yiddish expressions and each time, Jerry and Leonard exchanged funny glances and even Father Bernie lifted his eyebrows and cocked his balding head. At one point, she held her head and yelled, "Gevalt! I forgot the serve the Jell-O mold." The brothers laughed out loud. "It's all right, Mom." Leonard said. "No biggie, Gram," Haley said and high fived Heidi. Something out of my reach had been going on and I wanted to know.

After the family staggered from the table filled with cheesecake and coffee or tea, we moved to the living room to sit for a little while. I needed fresh air and a walk to the next county. Maybe Indiana.

A photo album on the coffee table called to me. In large gold print I read Jerome Kahn Bar Mitzvah. I finally got it. Mrs. Kahn's big show of Jewish life and I bet she never acted like that in real life. She must be afraid and I didn't want her to be worried about her son with me.

"Mom, you really went all out with dinner tonight and everything was beautiful. Just one little question. You never say the blessing in Hebrew and you never use Yiddish expressions so why did you feel tonight you had to work so hard at being Jewish?" Jerry said.

Sophie looked around the room at all her loved ones. *Not me.* "I did?"

"Duh," the twins said. "You did."

Bernie nodded, Leonard cleaned his glasses—*must be a family habit*; Elaine said nothing.

"Mrs. Kahn," I said, "I'm the outsider here. Jerry means the world to me. I promise I'm no threat to you and your family just because I've been raised differently. Jerry loves all of you. I never want to interfere with that. I'd rather join your team than break it up."

If we were in a movie, the credits would roll, applause, applause and The End flashes across the screen. Life isn't a movie. I knew when Jerry hurried to my side for a major hug and promise of more, like all couples we'd have good times and some hurdles to jump over. I knew how to jump hurdles better than anyone in the room. *Super Charlie.*

We said goodnight.

Sophie came to the door. "Sorry, I had an attack of the crazies. I'll work on it."

On the way to my house, Jerry opened the sun roof for fresh air. "So what do think about my family?"

"Oy, Vey!" I said.

Chapter 32

Murphy's Law got me.

Nothing is as easy as it looks and everything takes longer than you think

On the other hand, if I'd been busy with The Haven project, Mr. Duffy would have turned to Mike Connor to head up his next job instead of me. Chest pains and a warning from his doctor to slow down came at the opportune time. *Funny thing.* Content as foreman, Mike didn't want total responsibility and I did. With Jimmy about to graduate high school, he said he'd learn from Mike. Jerry, my right hand everything handled the business end. Uncle suggested we call the business C. Stuart Construction.

"Men believe men are better in this type of business. You have been seen on the backhoe. A picture appeared in the paper, as I recall. The caption read 'Charlie Costigan, the girl on the backhoe.' What do you think, Charlie?"

I tried it out. Picked up the phone and said, "Good morning, C. Stuart Construction." "Good. Order cards," I said, and I did. C. Stuart Construction was now officially in business. I needed to hire someone to answer phones. Not my job.

Mr. Duffy said okay to the name change. He wanted to retire and fish and asked if I'd be able to buy him out over a period of time.

"Get Stuart over here for a meet. We'll talk some business."

"This is what I've dreamed about since the day I walked in. Are you positive, Mr. Duffy?"

"Oh yeah. My ticker's telling me something not to be ignored. I'll call my old friend and we can figure something workable for you, young lady. How old are you?"

Why did this always come up? "Twenty two."

He laughed the gravelly laugh I'd miss. "It's about time."

After meeting with the owners of the property who wanted a family compound built, I knew why Mr. Duffy opted out.

Another cold winter day, March wind blowing off the lake, Jimmy, Mike Connor and I drove to what appeared to be a three acre prime piece of real estate tucked back in the woods in close to Wilmette, Illinois. Mr. and Mrs. Flynn Doyle insisted we be there promptly at nine in the morning. We were there well before to have time to stomp around, check the terrain, be aware of problems. And there were many.

Ignoring me, Jimmy conferred with Mike. "This is a topographical nightmare. You got your highs up here on this end, sandy soil down here, trees from the Stone Age rooted everywhere and walls of pulverized rock fused together. How are we gonna clear enough space to build three houses?" Jimmy said.

"We'll figure it out. I sure hope they're easy to work with," Mike said.

I listened, watched steam curl from my hot tea cup and hoped the Doyle's showed up soon.

A Hummer buzzed through the woods and out stepped Cruella Deville. I mean Mrs. Doyle. Swathed in what looked like real jaguar skins, she carried two yappy Yorkshire Terriers one under each furry pit, hers not theirs. They were a perfect snack size for Lord and Lady to share. She herself resembled an endangered species. Gliding toward the men, she stopped in front of my handsome kid brother Jimmy.

"Well hello, cowboy. You've come to survey my property?" A throaty laugh followed. Jimmy grinned. Mike's face turned red. She ignored me.

A portly man bustled over, shook hands with the men, and checked out my tight jeans. "C Alfred Construction?" We all said yes. "I'm Flynn Doyle. My wife," he gestured to the coat now bending over the tiny dogs urging them to do what they were going to do no matter what she said. "Well, what do you think? Beautiful, yes?"

I took over assuming he referred to the land and not Mrs. Doyle's backside. "Yes. It's a wonderful property." Taking him by the arm, we carefully tread over roots meant to kill or maim and treacherous rocks threatening to bean one or both of us in the head. "There are numerous topographical problems to be addressed but nothing we can't avoid with careful planning. Jim is an excellent architect and Mike is my best foreman with years of experience. We'll try as best we can to meet your expectations."

"And who are you, young lady?"

"I'm Charlie Costigan, CEO. C. Stuart Construction."

"What happened to Duffy?"

"Sadly, Mr. Duffy became ill and had to retire. I worked with him all through college, Northwestern, and when I graduated he offered me a deal. I couldn't refuse."

"Wait a minute. Are you the Costigan cross country winner?"

"That I am. Proud to be a member of the team. Building is my calling, Mr. Doyle. We'll do a good job for you."

Walking back to my guys and the fur thief, I pointed out numerous obstacles we'd have to overcome. I didn't know then, on that blustery cold morning, Mrs. Doyle would be the worst obstacle. Betsy Doyle could suck the juice out of your day if you let her. Jimmy held the dog leads and looked like a chump. I'd have to keep him on a short leash from this man eater. Mike, too. Oh Angie. Being the boss lady would be a whole 'nother business.

After that inauspicious beginning, we met with Betsy Doyle far too often. She knew her blueprints; got out the reading glasses to pour over every line Jimmy had meticulously drawn. And he had the touch and instinct to carve out of the monster acreage an interesting concept of three homes.

Then she brought in the experts, the Doyle children, recipients of two houses, also experts. Just ask them. Both daughters were debutantes, newly married after coming out to society the year before. I stifled a laugh when hearing of the parties and gowns. Aunt Eleanor and Uncle Stuart offered to present me to society when I reach eighteen. I preferred the Thunderbird and giving back to the community on my own. The daughters resembled Tom Donnelly's Muffy girlfriends with long straight blond hair and thin frames. I wondered about Tom, maybe he married a Muffy but no. He had another year to go for law school.

A new demand came in from the Doyle's. A tennis court and is there room for a stable? I let the guys sort out the little stuff while Jerry and I worked on the business end. Mrs. Doyle kept complaining about the trailer we'd inherited from Mr. Duffy. Even though it had been moved to her property, she objected to the worn appearance. They had big bucks and we aimed to please so I had the guys paint the outside and a landscaper brought potted bushes to soften the look. For now, we privately called our place of business The No-Tell-Motel.

Jerry wanted a real city office for me. Something special to bring potential clients to. I liked a trailer, crammed with workers coming and going. We had to make a compromise. One starry night in May, just after my twenty third birthday, Jerry surprised me. After passing the CPA exam, he opened an office on Michigan Avenue. His father had semi-retired and Jerry took over old accounts and the business grew. Now he hired a small staff of young accountants. This night, his dark eyes sparkled after taking me to a favorite piano bar where fresh fish was the specialty. "Play me a song, you're the Piano man," sang the pianist and Jerry rolled a five dollar bill to place in a glass on the piano. We loved the old Billy Joel songs.

Leaving the restaurant, Jerry steered me across the Magnificent Mile to his building, waved to the guard and up we went to the fifteenth floor. "I want to show you something special," Jerry said.

Jerome Kahn and Bernard Kahn Associates etched in gold on the left side of the double doors. Emblazoned on the right door C. Stuart Construction.

An office of my own. I couldn't believe it. "Follow me," he said.

"I'll follow you anywhere," I said and meant it.

We walked on plush gold tweed carpet past cubicles for his staff and came to a carved walnut door with a plaque again declaring my space. He handed me a key. The door opened to a large corner room overlooking the avenue, complete with an old fashioned roll top desk, conference table, leather visitor's chairs, a couch and a small private bathroom.

"Jerry, what can I say?"

"How about yes?"

"Will you do the little kisses on my fingers and hands again?"

He removed his glasses and set them on my new/old desk. "Maybe."

His tie came off. He said, "Oh, all right."

"Will we love and cherish each other forever?"

Unbuttoning his shirt, he said, "We already do."

"And no harsh words. Always communicate. Promise?"

I stepped out of my dress and kicked off my sandals.

"I promise."

"I'm a virgin."

We kissed until my strong legs grew weak. "So am I," Jerry said. "We waited for us."

Jimmy wanted to be my maid of honor or flower girl. He tossed a coin with Edgar. Robert won. The house filled with laughter every day. Shelley won maid of honor and brought guess who—Patrick. The Kahn's had too many friends and relatives, our garden couldn't hold so many people. We considered two ceremonies—one for Jerry's side, one for mine. All in good fun. Eloping became an option and vetoed. What to do. I went for a long run. Jerry followed on his bike and we allowed the seniors to decide. By the time we returned, the plans were set.

Our marriage took place in the garden at the place I'd called home since 1996. A rabbi and a priest took turns in a beautiful ceremony. *Religion in stereo surround sound. The in-laws and out-laws. My imagination went wild.* I moved in with Jerry in a building he'd purchased a couple years before. Renovated recently by C. Stuart Construction, it became an ad for suburban living in the city.

Meanwhile, north in Wilmette, Betsy Doyle alternated between going for my brother and Mike as if she had dual personalities or just had an itch that needed scratching. A lot. I warned both of them it could lead to trouble. The property alone required concentration. The daughter's homes were basically the same. Jim designed them to what he called flop over so they wouldn't look alike, with fieldstone and wood outside giving a rugged appearance to fit in with the existing land.

The main house needed to be a McMansion according to Betsy. Fancy and big. Lots of marble and columns. A wrap around portico. Maybe she came from a deprived background and tried to make up for it. I don't know. Jimmy had a way with her though and slowly, he convinced her that less is more. If he showed her the way in some bedroom, I didn't care by now. The job bore our stamp and I wanted it to be worthy. Betsy seemed calmer, had a glow that didn't come from her devoted husband. Yes. Must be brother Jim. He deserved a bonus.

Before Halloween, to my relief the Doyle project ended. The crew and I celebrated with a fine party of steaks, ribs and all the fixings. I began a tradition of gift giving to my customers. A special boulder rolled in place or an exotic indoor plant.

As we moved the trailer and equipment from the site, neighbors stopped to ask for business cards and to shake my calloused hand. Jobs would come from this pain in the butt. I'd learned a lot in business and best of all, I got married. *Mom, do you ever think of me?*

Chapter 33

2005

The Haven project slowed for too long a time. With the house almost ready for a family, I needed to make things happen. After months of meetings, we all realized the endowment idea needed work. Legal attention. The Anderson's insisted I come to their office in Fairview. With Robert unavailable, the Thunderbird and I made the trip north without a hitch and found a parking place in front of an architectural wonder. This time I dressed like the CEO I'd become. Four inch heels weren't meant to climb crumbling steps. With my new grown-up status, I thought about law suits and wondered if Brent and Grace Anderson had coverage and should I mention it to them.

A grizzled old man checked my I.D. and looked as if he wanted to frisk me. *Oh no you don't Pops.* I said the magic word Anderson and he let me pass me pointing to swinging doors just ahead. Careful not to let one hit me in the ass, I entered the noisiest space I'd ever been in outside of a stadium. The acoustics were awful and no one cared but sensitive little me with everyone at computers, phones and all kinds of newspaper stuff going on. Fast. The receptionist grabbed my arm, said, "Charlie Costigan?" mumbled something about expecting a guy and opened the door to an inner sanctum of beauty and quiet.

Blueprints of the addition I'd discussed with Kirk and Carly were spread out on a table. A couple I guessed were Brent and Grace, sat hip to hip on a long desk carved from the most gorgeous single piece of wood I had seen so far. Dressed almost like twins, they looked like matching book ends.

"Hello, Charlie," he said, "we've heard. . ."

"so much about you," Grace finished.

Oh, they finished each other's sentences. The conversation went on, friendly with many questions and they spoke about the endowment. Their law firm had someone who would set up an endowment plan.

RECONSTRUCTING CHARLIE

Their unusual way of speaking began to make me dizzy and when Bruce mentioned words like tax exempt, I tuned out. *Not my bag, folks. Jerry and Uncle knew. Not me.* The Anderson's were the oddest couple I'd ever met yet they had the indefinable quality together I admired of love and sweetness. And later, as we had almost the best chocolates ever, Aunt Eleanor's were better, they bounced back and forth before saying they were friends since childhood with Kirk. And to add to the mix, Carly used to work at their newspaper where she met Kirk who later left the church and married her. *Sounded like daytime drama to me.*

Again, in case I didn't get it the first time, I heard about this lawyer who had to set up a tax situation and again, I tuned out.

"I am concerned about some family somewhere right now, in need of help. Isn't there a way to speed things up?" I said.

"Charlie, everything takes time. Please be patient. Meanwhile, Brent and Grace have allotted money to furnish your existing home. And Carly has agreed to lend her expertise in getting the best deal."

Delighted finally something moved forward and grateful for generosity, I thanked them all and stood up, stretched to the ceiling forgetting I wore heels and a suit. "Oops. Sorry. I've spent years wearing track suits and now I'm in heels, off balance."

"You clean up very well," Kirk said.

I shook hands with Brent and Grace and couldn't resist giving a hug to Kirk and Carly for their kindness and patience. "How do you like the plans for an addition? My brother Jimmy designed it."

"Exceptional," Bruce said, all by himself. "We'll keep. . ."

"you informed about the lawyer," Grace said.

Carly said, "If you don't have to rush back, now's a good time to go to a model home and maybe get a good deal on furniture."

"Okay. I'm a fast shopper. Let's do it." I followed her to a gated community where a model home sale was to begin the following day. The gatekeeper waved us in. "Wait 'til you see this stuff. I've had my eye on it and the seller expects me today before the crowd."

Carly Richards had the eye all right. Durable playroom furniture, sensible attractive living room and dining room sets, and every bedroom would do. She said, "Let me do the talking, bargaining if you will, and in one fell swoop or swell foop, you'll have a house decorated and ready. The key word is long lasting and durable."

"Uh, right. Be my guest." She had the checkbook and good taste. I allowed Carly to take the burden off my shoulders and we used the Anderson gift to good advantage.

"They can deliver tomorrow at nine a.m. We live close by. Kirk and I can meet you and help set up. Is that okay?"

"Well, yes and thanks. It's more than I expected, Carly."

"Hey, is this a wedding band?" she said.

"Yes." I twisted the ring around my finger and felt the magic thrill of my husband's touch. "Jerry and I got married. He's my forever sweetheart."

She hugged me. "My best to you both. Kirk will be very happy to know you have someone special in your life."

My new best friends were busy moving furniture when I arrived at The Haven the next morning. Autumn leaves fell fast as the chilly wind blew them from their hold on the trees. A little curly haired blond gathered leaves with care as if they were treasures. When I stepped out of my car, she made her way over to me, gazing up into my eyes all the time. Blue magnetic eyes so compelling, I couldn't break away. Kneeling down to her size, I said, "Hi." Solemn, she handed me two golden leaves. Her warm soft palms pressed my face. "Pertector, Charlie."

"Do you mean protector?" She nodded, serious and wise. "Like I'm a protector?" Again her curls bobbed up and down. *I'd been a protector of my family since childhood in Minnesota and continued to have the need to protect. The Haven cried out to nourish needy families. How did this child know so much about me?*

"Who are you?" I said.

"PattiRea Jensen. I'm four." She held up four chubby fingers.

"How do you know my name?"

A shrug of small shoulders, a sly smile and she scampered off calling, "I just know. Ask Granny."

A few long strides and I scooped her up in my arms. We entered the house. Placing a finger against my mouth, PattiRea said, "Shh. Listen to the house."

I did. Underneath sounds created by Kirk and Carly shifting furniture in the living room, I picked up on sighs and maybe laughter. "What is it?" I whispered.

"Happy." She wriggled loose and ran to find her Granny and Kirk.

Happy? Hmm. A house with happy.

"You're not finished? I planned coming late to avoid working," I said. The living room shaped up just as we'd pictured. Cozy and comfortable. "And I found the perfect centerpiece for the coffee table."

PattiRea leapt into my arms and I balanced her on top of a wide stack of books. "Tada," she said, arms spread wide, one foot tucked in a passé like a balance beam pose. Then she sat, engrossed in the top book, reading with great expression.

The three of us stopped for coffee in the kitchen, out of hearing range from small ears. "About your granddaughter. She has a gift, right? She knows me, knows I'm what she calls a protector. She said this house is happy, told me to listen and I heard sounds. Good sounds. Sighs of pleasure and laughter." I blinked back a lifetime of tears talking to them. They listened, drank coffee, nibbled on fresh pecan rolls. I bit into the most delicious flaky roll, dunked it my sweet milky coffee and ate some more. "Tell me about this amazing kid and what this all means."

Kirk nodded to Carly. "Go on, love."

"PattiRea is psychic in many ways. She senses the past and future. Either she'll grow out of it or her power will grow stronger. No way to know. A few years ago, when she was an infant, I told her I loved Kirk. The following year, she said he'd come back." They exchanged one of those glances I'd seen before. "She warned me about someone months before I met him and she was maybe a year old. Lately her predictions have been homebound about her twin sisters and the new baby sister. PattiRea is a mistress of anticipation. Also, she sees my mother every so often and my first husband visits her. Both died a while back." Carly reached for Kirk's hand. "She knew Bob approved of Kirk just the way my dogs did."

"Dogs?"

"Two old dogs. A Shepherd and a Lab."

"I have two Labradoodles who know me inside and out and they love Jerry."

A jeep rumbled to the front, braked and stopped. "Yee Haw," came the familiar cry from Jimmy. Two doors slammed and Jerry said, "Where's my wife?"

I laughed and ran to greet them. The cowpoke/architect and the CPA/lover man of my life.

PattiRea beat me to the door, a cross country star in the making.

"Are you the lady of the house?" Jimmy said, hunkering down to face her.

"Charlie's brother, you." She leaned her forehead against his. "Be good." Jimmy frowned.

"Hello, I'm Charlie's husband, Jerry. Who are you?" I stayed back to watch my guy in action.

"PattiRea Jensen. I'm four." Trusting, she slipped her small hand in his and led him into the happy house. A good sign.

"What did she mean?" Jimmy said. "And who is she?"

"Brother, if PattiRea Jensen tells you to be good, listen. I'll explain more later."

By mid-afternoon with the house in order, we headed back to the city. Kirk said he'd be on the lookout for our first family. Halfway home, Grace Anderson called. She had a lawyer for the endowment and a meeting scheduled the following day in my office at eleven. I had power of attorney and as much as I wanted to tune out, my grown-up time had arrived.

Chapter 34

Pacing back and forth in new black leather boots with stiletto heels is not my idea of smarts. I vowed to kick the damn things off as soon as the lawyer left. I paused, looked out at the city below and breathed. *So you're not in your best comfort zone with the tax exempt thing and endowment but there is an office full of people who can come to the rescue, if need be. You are the CEO, Chairman of the Board, lady. Fake it. You know everything else.*

The intercom buzzed. "Your eleven o'clock is here."

Showtime. "Thanks. Send him down."

Before I had time to reach my desk, the door opened. Thomas Donnelly walked in. The old grin spread across his handsome face. "I have an appointment with C. Stuart. What are you doing here?"

"Hello, Tom. Good to see you, too." I sat at my desk and gestured to one of the visitor's chairs. "When Grace and Brent Anderson called about the endowment and said a lawyer would be coming today, they didn't mention your name." I searched for an appropriate smile, found one and used it. Tom fumbled through his attaché case for a folder, not quite the smooth moves of the Tom I'd once known and cared for. Placing the papers in front of me, he began to explain. I held up my hand, pressed #2 and called George Elias. Let him earn his money while I watched and listened. George barreled in, a former wrestler at NU and an expert with Jerry's company. After the introduction, we sat at the conference table where, in one billable hour, the work ended. Papers signed and notarized, George excused himself and left.

"You are Charlie Costigan, right?"

"Yes and CEO of C. Stuart Construction the past two years. The Haven is a project I had in mind and now with the help of the Anderson's and several other sponsors, my dream will come true."

Tom's blond hair showed streaks of gray. I did a quick calculation. He's only about twenty six and already frown wrinkles marred his former perfection. "So you accomplished your plan of becoming a lawyer. Congratulations."

I couldn't wait for him to leave, wondered what I'd ever seen in him and yet he moved around the office reading my awards, touching trophies, a look of regret on his face.

"Is something wrong, Tom?"

He glanced around the office with all of my accomplishments displayed one last time and shook his head. "No." At the door, he turned back. "You gave back to the community in a big way. I read about it, thought then what a fool you were for wasting precious time while I concentrated on my career, my women, myself." The once golden boy with so much promise didn't appear to be quite so golden. "Yes, I'm a lawyer and yes I have my share of women and clients but you're the winner with the enriched life. I should have been patient, Charlie. You were worth waiting for."

The intercom buzzed. "Your husband's back."

"Send him down."

"Husband?"

Joy spread through my body just to hear the word. "Yes, Jerry Kahn and I got married."

The next time a lawyer came with business from Brent and Grace, it wasn't Tom.

No matter how old you are, sometimes a girl needs her mother. For me, mother meant Aunt Eleanor. I called, made an appointment for a personal conference, just the two of us. Of course, two became three when Uncle Stuart got wind of it and before we finished, Jimmy, who still lived with them, got in the act.

We sat in the garden room one spring day, Aunt Eleanor and I, in private conversation. "What's on your mind, dear?" Aunt said.

"Almost ten years ago, I knocked on your door. You're the mother I never had but Aunt Eleanor, I have unfinished business with her, the mother who sent me to you, and now I have to see her one more time to put it to rest."

"You want to go to Utah?"

"Yes. To look her right in the eyes and ask why. Why she sent me away and never called. Why birthdays passed and graduations and now I'm married. . ." *Breathe, Charlie.*

Uncle Stuart walked in. "Go where?"

"Charlie wants to see Elizabeth. Ten years have passed and she never once contacted our girl. Just sent her away to us not knowing what would become of our wonderful girl."

"And what do you expect to find when you see her, Charlie?" Uncle Stuart said.

I shook my head. "I don't know. But I need to face her and ask."

Their worried faces searched mine. "Jerry is all in favor of me going. To satisfy myself. Then I can get on with my life. See, she's like a missing puzzle, a part of me long gone. Then maybe I can shed the skin that binds me to her."

"To who?" Jimmy said, striding in without knocking.

"Charlie's going to Utah to see her mother and have a confrontation," Uncle Stuart said.

"No dear. She wants to satisfy herself that she's not missing something and also ask Elizabeth why she's been so disinterested in her for ten years."

"I'm going with you, Sis. Not because you can't go alone. But just because I want to be there when you look at our mother and see nothing. She gave birth to us. That's all. The rest is air."

"And the twins?" I said.

"They're toast. She's got them churched up and that's where they'll stay. When do you want to go?"

"Right away."

A week later, my brother and I hurried off the plane in Salt Lake City so eager to get to our destination, we didn't take time to breathe the dry air Jimmy had talked about or check out the scenery.

"Nice day," I said as Jimmy turned the car around and headed to the highway.

"Uh huh. Good day to see the twins."

"Twins? I thought we'd see Mom first and visit the girls on the way to the airport."

"Better this way. Trust me."

RECONSTRUCTING CHARLIE

We munched on apples and drove up winding road to a secluded private school about an hour from Mom's place. All around us, eagles swooped down from the cloudless blue sky on unsuspecting prey. *Just like human life.* Sounds of laughter came from behind a tall fence. "Must be recreation time," Jimmy said. "Very strict here. I'll flash my pearly whites and bat my lashes. Maybe we can get in."

"Why don't you just ask?"

"That, too," Jimmy said.

When all his charms failed to get the Sister in charge to open the door, I stepped up to the plate. I handed her my business card. "My name is Charlie Costigan. Celia and Cary are our twin sisters and I haven't seen them in ten years. I would appreciate so much your allowing us to visit with them. Our flight leaves in two hours."

Sister Margaret Mary smiled, her young face pleasant and eager to please. The door opened wide. We were in. My pulse raced and Jimmy whispered, "Good job, Sis."

"The girls are at outdoor activities now. We don't like them to be interrupted."

"What kind of activities?"

"They run, exercise, you know." She glanced at both of us. "You are both fit so you understand how important it is to your good health."

And what about a loving home? Dates and being a kid? Or doesn't that count here?

The gate opened, a ball flew in my direction. I caught it and ran as fast as I could in tight jeans and running shoes and threw it to someone waving her arms. She caught it and laughed a familiar laugh. We stopped, looked and ran into each other's arms.

"Celia?"

"No. Cary. You're our Charlie!" She yelled, "Celia, it's Charlie."

Jimmy loped over. "Hey, what am I, chopped liver?" They didn't get it. They lived in Utah, after all. But we all hugged and had a real family reunion.

The girls were okay with the school, unsure if a religious future was what they wanted. We gave them phone and address contacts, assured them our lives were good in Chicago and after looking around, Jimmy and I decided the school seemed to be an okay place for now. In the few moments left, I told them about our special aunt and uncle who gave me a home ten years before.

Jimmy said, "When I left here, Aunt Eleanor and Uncle Stuart made room for me. Now Charlie and I work together. Think about it, sisters, and know we love you."

Goodbyes are never easy. At best, our sixteen year old sisters, Celia and Cary had each other.

Jimmy drove the rented car, maneuvering his way 'til we came to a pull off road with a painted wood sign. RIDE the RANCH Vacations Day & Weekly tours. C'mon in.

We followed the big black arrow. "Stop while I catch my breath, little bro."

"Pretty, isn't it?" Jim said.

I looked around and saw mountains everywhere ready to gobble you up and spit out your bones. Accustomed to the flatlands and cornfields not far from Chicago, the mountains crowded me.

Clutching my brother's powerful bicep, I said, "This will be the shortest trip. I promise. One look and it's over."

His eyes sparkled. "Yeah."

Bouncing along the dusty unpaved road, glad we rented an SUV, we drove up to a large log cabin one story rustic house. So this was Max Calhoun's spread. I hopped out, steadied my nerves for the unexpected visit and my faithful companion joined me, tense and ready to spring.

"Calm down and focus," I said.

A woman dressed in a checkered shirt, blue jeans and boots, cowboy hat with gray hair braided blowing in the wind, cantered across the big field on a tall dark brown horse with a white star of mane on his forehead.

"My horse," Jim said.

From a distance, she waved and called, "Howdy. Be right there."

She dismounted, her eyes never leaving mine, and handed the reins to Jimmy. He reached into a barrel next to the house and fed carrots to his horse.

"Hey, Charlie. Hey Jimbo. How are you?"

RECONSTRUCTING CHARLIE

Mother, daughter, son caught in a moment of time. I wanted to shake Mom, grab her by her bony shoulders and shake her until she rattled like dear old Dad's skeleton must rattle. All I did was what I came to do. Just look deep in her eyes the same color as mine. Memories of that defining night in my young life flashed again. I always protected her and she knew it. He always came home drunk Friday nights and I was there. The porcelain egg broke, she must have cried out for me to help so I did what Mom had trained me to do. Strong and capable fifteen year old Charlie Costigan grabbed the tire iron and killed for her. I set her free and what did Mom do? She threw me away like disposable garbage, my usefulness over. How fortunate for me Mom's sister opened her arms to welcome me into the best of all possible worlds.

"Let's go Jimmy. I have what I came for."

He stroked his horse one last time.

Mom examined her boots and never looked up.

We Costigan kids grew up fast and now we were a family again. Jimmy and I high-fived at the airport. I waited at the gate while he turned in the car. My cell phone rang. I moved to a quiet place.

"Charlie, it's Kirk Richards. I have a family for The Haven. I'm at the hospital now. It's bad."

"I'm in Salt Lake City. I'll be back in about six hours. Call Shelley Jackson."

"We'll see you soon. God speed."

Book Club Discussion Starters
Reconstructing Charlie
By Charmaine Gordon

- Forced to leave home at fifteen, Charlie Costigan begins a new life. Can you picture yourself in a similar situation and would you have the courage to survive?

- She carries a terrible secret shared only with her mother. Is it too much a burden for a person to carry the rest of her life or should she seek counsel when her mother moves away and loses touch?

- When the high school track team plays dirty, she deals with them in her own way without telling the coach. Do you admire her attitude or would you have brought the authorities in believing they'd get faster action.

- In a time of sexual freedom of both sexes, can you appreciate her old fashioned belief in the importance of virginity?

- Tom Donnelly, the football player who wants more than Charlie is willing to give, walks away choosing instead a succession of socialites. Will he regret his loss?

- She is a planner, always looking toward her next move. Building/constructing has special meaning for her. The concept of creating something strong and durable as compared to the flimsy egg shells her family walked on with the threat of violence at every turn. Do you approve of her career choice motivated by such a background?

- Jerry Kahn, the young man she slowly bonds with, works with numbers and business. Can you see a lasting relationship to their union despite religious difference?

- When Charlie meets the elderly man in the house deep in the woods, she finds a spiritual connection and begins building The Haven. Does a place like this exist in real life?

- Brother Jimmy Costigan joins Charlie and both are embraced by the wonderful Aunt Eleanor and Uncle Stuart. An interesting hot guy, is Jimmy someone you'd like to read more about?

- Labradoodles play an important part in the story, two puppies arriving in the quiet elegant home the same day Charlie shows up. Do you like to read about pets in a story.

- The household staff also are provocative characters. We learn about Robert's background. Edgar would make some interesting chapters and Sean and his girlfriend Sarah-can you see a married life for a Down Syndrome couple?

More Great Books by Charmaine Gordon

The Catch

    Tom Donnelly, once known as The Catch – every woman's dream guy, has fallen down every rung of the ladder he once worked so hard to climb. On New Year's Day, he realizes just how far he's fallen, and makes a list of resolutions to change his life. He vows to regain the trust lost from his family, his law firm, and his friends – and maybe even find the right woman this time.

Sin of Omission

    A twist of fate intervenes when Shelley keeps a secret that threatens to break apart the Costigans and her future. A mysterious client, Deanna Rose, enters Haven, victim of a savage beating under strange circumstances. Shelley investigates and finds Ms. Rose has an unsavory past. With the reputation and safety of Haven at stake, Shelley is at risk to lose everything and everyone she cares about.

Reconstructing Charlie

Charlie Costigan has a secret. Home life gone from bad to the worst when she protects her mother from another vicious attack by her drunken father. Midnight. Clothes thrown into an old suitcase, she races for the bus with a letter to an unknown aunt and uncle. "This is my daughter. Embrace her as if she were your own." Determined, Charlie begins again. Alone with her secret.

Now What?

I held his cooling hand and asked the two words spoken many times during our years together. "Now what?" This time there was no response. I was on my own for the first time. When my fingers touched his wedding ring, I slipped it off and held it in my fist. The gold band was warm. I clung to him. "Come back to me, dearest." Sometimes what you wish for is more than you can live with.

Starting Over

Each morning, Emily Kendrick runs on the hard-packed sand of St. Augustine Beach to clear her mind and heal her heart. From the widow's walk of the house perched high on the dunes, a man trains his binoculars on Emily...

 **ALSO IN AUDIOBOOK!**

To Be Continued

Elizabeth Malone wakes up the morning after an amazing night of passion with her husband of forty years to find a note: Dear Lizzie, it's not you, it's me. Abandoned by her husband, disappointed in daughter Susie's casual attitude Dad's having a mid-life crisis, Beth decides to re-establish herself as the winner she once was. When Frank Malone returns, he's in for a big surprise!

And her most recent series...

The Beginning... Not the End

Charmaine Gordon writes books about women who Survive and Thrive. Her motto is take one step and then another to leave your past behind and begin again. Six books and several short stories in three years, she's always at work on the next story. The books include *To Be Continued*, *Starting Over*, *Now What?*, *Reconstructing Charlie*, *Sin of Omission* and *The Catch*, just released.

"I didn't realize at the time while working as an actor in NYC, I'd become a sponge soaking up dialogue, setting, and stage directions. I learned many tools of writing during the years watching directors like Mike Nichols and actors including Harrison Ford, Anthony Hopkins, and Billy Crystal. And would you believe, I was Geraldine Ferraro's stand-in leg model, my first job giving me entrée into all the Unions needed to work. When the sweet time ended, I began another career and creative juices flowed."

You can reach Charmaine at
http://authorCharmaineGordon.wordpress.com

And on her FB page
http://www.facebook.com/charmaine.gordon